The String Book of Ron Leys, Journalist

RON LEYS, JOURNALIST

authorHOUSE®

AuthorHouse™
1663 Liberty Drive
Bloomington, IN 47403
www.authorhouse.com
Phone: 833-262-8899

Published by AuthorHouse   05/10/2023

ISBN: 978-1-7283-7705-6 (sc)
ISBN: 978-1-7283-7704-9 (hc)
ISBN: 979-8-8230-0526-5 (e)

Library of Congress Control Number: 2023908705

Print information available on the last page.

Any people depicted in stock imagery provided by Getty Images are models, and such images are being used for illustrative purposes only. Certain stock imagery © Getty Images.

This book is printed on acid-free paper.

BACK IN THE DAY, MANY REPORTERS AND COLUMNISTS KEPT A folder or big envelope in a desk drawer. Whenever he or she wrote something that might impress a future prospective employer, it was clipped and saved in this folder or envelope. This was known as a string book.

The phrase was borrowed from the common term for free-lance writers, who were paid by the column inch of published material. They were known as stringers, from the old practice of pasting together their published stories in sort of a string, which could then be measured and submitted for payment, monthly or otherwise. Staffers, on the other hand, were paid by the week, or for part-timers, by the hour.

In the fall of 1959, an English professor at the University of Wisconsin suggested that I consider becoming a professional writer. My career thus far had included a hitch in the United States Navy, followed by several years as a construction worker and truck driver.

Just before my GI Bill eligibility expired, I enrolled at the UW. Taking the professor's advice, I majored in journalism. I met a fellow journalist, Marilyn Shapiro, and we married.

During the summer of 1961 I interned at The Rockford Morning Star in northern Illinois.

On completion of college, I became a full time reporter there.

In 1969, I went to work for The Milwaukee Journal. I worked as a copy editor, reporter, nature columnist, suburban editor, and outdoor editor.

I retired in 1991, although I wrote freelance columns for the

Journal's Sunday magazine, and later for an independent magazine, The Wisconsin Outdoor Journal.

When that ended, it was over. It turned out that I only wrote for the money. When they stopped paying me. I stopped writing. Although it probably had more to do with losing an audience. That was always the point, writing for readers.

Bear on Leash, Elephant Ride End Dreams of Relaxing Day at Circus

By RON LEYS
Morning Star Staff Writer

August 2, 1962

ALKING TO CLOWNS, EATING COTTON CANDY AND HOT DOGS, watching the performers and the animals, all on a free pass to the Clyde Brothers Shrine Circus, make for an afternoon.

All that I did Wednesday . . . all that and then some I hadn't reckoned on.

Like strolling along at the corner of State and Main Sts. with a bear as a companion, or taking a ride on an elephant at Beyer Stadium, where the circus opened its three-day stand.

I had heard that there would be some trained bears showing off in downtown Rockford at noon, so I went to take a look.

When the bears arrived in a pickup truck, driven by their trainer, Wally Naghtin, there was one bear too many for Naghtin to lead, so he glanced at me and said, "Here, you take Connie and I'll lead Tuffy."

There didn't seem to be much choice, so I took the leash and led

1

her to the corner, where the bears spent 15 or 20 minutes entertaining a small crowd by roller-skating, standing on their front paws and clowning around.

I had heard that trained bears don't bite hard, but I still was glad Connie wore a muzzle.

Later at the circus grounds I saw Ed Akins, elephant trainer for the circus, sitting on the steps of the trailer he shares with his three elephants, Mary, Sue and Ruth.

The three elephants were standing nearby, munching hay and throwing dirt on their backs to keep the flies off.

We stood and talked about elephants and circuses and things. It was about an hour before show time. The performers and animals were taking it easy in the field behind the stadium.

No different than other boys, I always had dreamed of riding an elephant. I looked over at the animals and they didn't look so dangerous as they lazily scratched each other.

I casually asked Akins if I could ride one.

To my surprise, he said, "Sure."

He shouted, "Come here, Mary." Mary ambled over to Ed and me. Suddenly she looked about four times bigger than a mere seven feet. "Down, Mary." She grinned a little, and then slowly laid her huge body on the ground in front of us.

I put my left foot on her left leg, as Akins had told me. I stood there, not knowing what to do next. I looked at Akins and he said, "Just swing your right leg over her neck."

"Yeah, sure," I thought as I looked over that huge neck with its big flapping ears waving on each side. "Just like that."

I swallowed hard and swung. I gave a little jump, and found that I could straddle an elephant after all. Just barely, though.

There I sat, with both feet sticking out into space.

Akins shouted, "Up, Mary." She rolled to one side to get her feet under her. I was certain that she was going to roll all the way over with me underneath.

The rolling stopped and I could feel myself being pitched forward as she got her back end started up into the air. It was then that I realized that there is absolutely nothing to hold onto

on an elephant. There is no mane to grab and that loose skin isn't nearly as loose as it looks. Just as I was about to go over her head, the front end started up and Mary leveled out.

I felt mighty confident as she stood there, swaying slightly. Then she began to walk. Each time one of her legs went forward her neck on that side went down and I had to shift my weight desperately to the other side to keep from falling off. Then the other side would go down and I suddenly had to lean in the opposite direction.

After a few steps like that I sort of got the hang of it and Mary went ambling along, with me balanced on her back but I might as well confess Akins was alongside guiding her. I never had been told how to go about steering a hay-burner that big.

After I had gotten off, which was as treacherous a process as getting on, Mary strode off to join her girl friends, Ruth and Sue, under the trees about 200 yards from their trailer.

I sat and talked to Akins for a few minutes. He joined a carnival when he was 8, after he "got tired of a farm in Ohio." His first job was taking tickets for a sideshow, for which he was paid $1 a week.

He never saw his parents again.

A little later he got a job helping to take care of animals and has been working with circus animals ever since.

He began to train the three elephants as soon as they arrived from India in 1955. They were 3 years old at the time, just babies.

"They're like a family to me," Akins, who is 35, said proudly. "They are the only elephants in the world that are worked without an elephant hook. I treat them just like kids. When I call them, I expect them to come right over."

To demonstrate, he shouted at the top of his lungs, "Hey, Mary, Ruth, Sue! Come over here!"

Mary and Ruth shuffled over, but Sue had other ideas. She was munching on the leaves of a bush and paid no attention to her trainer. When Mary and Ruth saw that she wasn't going to join them, they added their trumpeting to Akins' shouting. Sue answered eagerly and came galloping over, grinning slyly. She looked a bit sheepish when Akins scolded her roundly.

"That Sue," he muttered, shaking his head like any exasperated parent, "she's got a mind of her own."

Ron Leys, staff reporter for the Morning Star, leads Connie, a trained black bear, down the sidewalk at W. State and Main Sts. Wednesday noon. Connie was in town with the Shrine-sponsored Clyde Brothers Circus now at Beyer Stadium.

Mary, a 10-year-old Indian elephant, raised her trunk to get a sniff at the stranger up on her back. Ed Akins, her trainer, gave Leys some much-needed advice on how to stay aboard. (Morning Star photos)

Alarm Rings; 22 Seconds Later, Firemen En Route

By RON LEYS
Morning Star Staff Writer

October 11, 1964

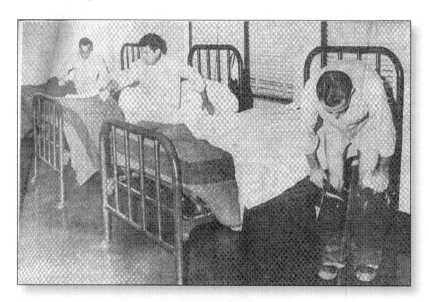

Firefighters: On Your Mark . . .

Firemen Raymond Schultz, left, John Lamendola, and Delbert "Bud" Rossier, right, are jarred out of their firehouse bunks by an alarm and take just seconds to jump into their waiting "bunker boots" and pants. (Morning Star photos)

7

*H*OW MUCH TIME ELAPSES BETWEEN THE SOUNDING OF A FIRE alarm and the rolling of the fire trucks?

Twenty-two seconds, if the firemen are all in bed when they hear the call.

That was the time clocked by Fire Chief Wayne Swanson during a special test conducted Thursday in Fire Station No. 2, Walnut and S. 1st Streets.

Swanson had the crews of the two trucks housed in the station — Engine 2 and Rescue Squad 1 — strip and take to their bunks, under the blankets.

Then the fire-alarm operator, Kenneth Keeling, announced over the loud speakers in the bunkroom there was a fire in the 200 block of N. 2nd Street.

The firemen leaped from their bunks and jumped into their "bunker boots." Their special trousers already were arranged over the boots in such a way that the fire fighters had only to pull up the pants and throw the suspenders over their shoulders to be fully dressed.

Since firemen always sleep in their underwear, shirts and socks — and need no shoes inside the felt-lined boots—they were ready to "hit the pole" just seconds after they heard the alarm.

The eight men swarmed down the brass pipe, hit the floor just behind their trucks, and jumped aboard, ready to put on their coats and helmets as the trucks rolled out the already - opened overhead doors.

Twenty-two seconds.

Was that unusually fast? Swanson said matter-of-factly that the time was about what he had expected

Would the eight men have taken longer if they had actually been sound asleep? Speaking from past experience as a rank-and-file fireman, Swanson said the time would have been about the same. Wake-up time is almost nil, he said.

SOMETIMES LONGER

He noted that it sometimes takes a few seconds longer for the trucks to roll for daylight alarms. He explained that fire truck crews often are scattered throughout the building when an alarm comes.

Any man who lags just a bit and doesn't make it to his truck when it is ready to roll is left behind in the firehouse, Swanson said.

"Then he's got to explain later why he was left."

Usually about eight to 10 minutes elapse between the time had alarm is sounded and the time water is being thrown on flames at the scene of a fire, according to Swanson.

The fire trucks roll through city streets at speeds between 30 and 40 miles an hour — although it seems faster to bystanders because the trucks are large and their sirens and unmuffled engines make a lot of noise.

45 SECONDS. . .

Once at the fire, the trucks hook up to the nearest hydrant and then drive slowly to the blaze, unreeling hose as they go. This usually takes about 45 seconds.

At small fires, they even save this time.

All fire engines have tanks of water aboard, and can spurt from 250 to 500 gallons of water without bothering to hook to a hydrant.

A few seconds are also taken by the fire alarm operator, who dispatches all trucks from Station 2. After a telephone call comes in, he often has to check files — kept at his fingertips — to determine which fire station is closest to the fire.

One man in each fire station stays awake all night on the main floor, just in case someone runs or drives up to the station to report a fire.

The men on each shift rotate this watch duty, and since firemen work for 24 hours and then are off-duty for 48 hours, standing the all-night watch doesn't come up often for any individual fireman.

WRONG IMAGE

The average person may have an image of the fireman as a lucky man who spends almost all of his time lounging and only works when there is a fire. But Swanson said this is not the case at all.

He noted that each fire truck is given a complete going-over after each "run" it makes. This includes washing even the underside of the truck, tightening up bolts and recharging equipment.

Firemen also are responsible for the cleanliness and upkeep of their stations. This duty includes scrubbing floors, washing walls, and cleaning windows, among the many other chores necessary to keep the stations spotless.

Training sessions also take up much of the men's time.

One veteran fireman noted that heart attacks are occupational hazards of firefighting.

"It puts a terrific strain on a man's heart to leap out of a sound sleep and immediately exert himself to his utmost," the old-timer said.

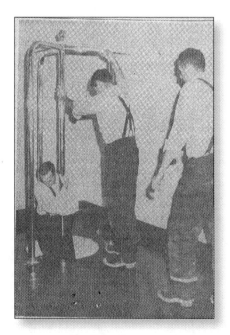

. . . Get Set . . .

One at a time, the fire fighters slide down the brass pole to the main floor, landing just behind their fire trucks.

. . . Go!

*Fully manned and ready for action, the fire truck rolls
out just 22 seconds after the alarm came in.*

Girl, 3, Perishes in Farm Fire

March 17, 1965

Dazed Father at Scene of Tragedy . . .

Standing in front of the blazing ruins of his parents' home, Earl Pettenger, left, tells of the fire which took the life of his daughter, Shirley, Tuesday. (Additional photo appears on page A10. Morning Star photo by Donald S. Holt)

Father's Frantic Rescue Try Fails Near Pecatonica

By RON LEYS
Morning Star Staff Writer

HREE-YEAR-OLD SHIRLEY LYNN PETTENGER PERISHED IN THE blazing home of her grandparents Tuesday evening as her father tried frantically to save her.

"I could hear her calling, but I couldn't get to her," her father, Earl Pettenger, said an hour later as he stared into the flickering flames of the leveled home.

Pettenger said he had eaten supper with his four small children in the quonset-type building he occupies next to the home of his parents, Mr. and Mrs. Raymond Pettenger, who live about three miles northwest of Pecatonica.

He left 5-year-old Joanne and 6-year-old Michael in their home, walked to his parents' house, and left Shirley and 7-year-old James there while he went to a barn to do the evening milking.

HEARS 'BOOM'

"About 10 minutes later, I heard a 'boom'," Pettenger said, "and I ran out of the barn. I saw Jimmie running out of the house, shouting, 'The house is on fire!'"

Pettenger ran to the back door, but was driven back by intense heat and smoke from inside the home. He ran to the side of the house and tried to open a bedroom window, but failed.

He finally got in through the front door and ran straight to a bedroom where he thought Shirley might be. Blinding smoke obscured everything.

"I felt around on the floor," he related, "but I couldn't find her."

Already burned by the searing heat, Pettenger broke out a bedroom window and escaped from the house.

He ran to a neighbor's farm and tried to call the Pecatonica Fire Department, but found phones in the area were knocked out.

Pecatonica Fire Chief Charles Moth explained later that the fire had short-circuited a several-party line which serves the area.

REPORTED BY NEIGHBOR

The fire was reported by Mrs. Menten Larson, who saw the leaping flames from her home about a mile away.

When firemen arrived, they found the building engulfed in flames. Under the streams of water, firefighters entered the home and found Shirley's body huddled under a bed.

Pettenger was taken to a doctor, where his burns were dressed. His surviving three children were taken in by neighbors.

The children's grandparents were away from home when the fire broke out. Pettenger's separated wife, Marie, lives in Freeport.

Chief Moth said he was unable immediately to determine what had caused the fire.

Believe Ex-Resident Murdered

January 17, 1965

Find Frozen Body Stuffed in Trunk Of Car in Elgin

By RON LEYS
Morning Star Staff Writer

A BODY TENTATIVELY IDENTIFIED AS THAT OF CHARLES LaFranka, 52, a former Rockford resident, was found in Elgin Saturday morning stuffed in the trunk of LaFranka's car.

LaFranka has not been seen since last Sunday afternoon when he was in Rockford visiting friends and relatives.

Elgin police said the dead man apparently had been beaten and strangled several days before. Kane County Coroner Victor Peterson said the body was frozen solid. An autopsy will be held today or Monday to determine the exact cause of death, he said.

LaFranka is an ex-convict, with a long record of arrests in Rockford.

HERE WEEK AGO

He had come to Rockford more than a week ago from Chicago, where he had been working, and was last seen here at 2 p.m. Sunday,

Jan. 10, several hours before he was due at the home of his parents, Mr. and Mrs. Joseph LaFranka, 719 Cunningham St.

He also failed to keep a date with a Rockford woman later that night.

Early Monday morning, his car was noticed parked in Elgin on E. Chicago Street near Chapel Street.

Charles LaFranka
. . . Visited here week ago

TRACED TO ROCKFORD

Rockford police were contacted, and it was found that the Rockford office of the Northern Illinois Corp. had a lien on the car.

The car was towed to a parking lot at the Elgin office of the loan firm.

Several days later, the loan firm called La Franka's brother, Ted LaFranka, in Denver. Also calling the brother was the Rockford woman who had had a date with LaFranka.

Ted LaFranka, who has been living in Denver under the name of "Ted Ross," called Elgin police Saturday morning and said he feared for the life of his brother, and suggested officers check the car's trunk.

A locksmith was called, and the locked trunk was opened.

LaFranka's body was found lying face-down. Police said marks on the body indicated LaFranka had been beaten and strangled.

LaFranka was dressed in a suit and overcoat and a comb was found in a pocket. Also found on the body were a ring and a watch.

Friends and relatives of the murdered man said Saturday that he had been living in Chicago for several years, and had visited Rockford from time to time. About a year ago, he spent several months in Rockford.

LaFranka's local police records begins in 1932. In June of that year, he was convicted of armed robbery and sentenced.

Police Trace La Franka's Final Hours in Rockford

OPERATING ON THE THEORY THAT CHARLES LAFRANKA, 52, MAY have been murdered in or near Rockford on Jan. 10 before his body was driven to Elgin in his car, Rockford police are tracing LaFranka's movements in Rockford on that date.

LaFranka's body was found last Saturday, stuffed into the trunk of his car, which had been spotted parked on a downtown Elgin street on Monday, Jan. 11.

Kane County Coroner L. Victor Peterson said a preliminary postmortem examination showed LaFranka had been slowly strangled to death, perhaps with a rope.

Rockford police said LaFranka arrived here shortly after noon on Jan. 10 and checked into the Flying Saucer Motel, 2004 11ᵗʰ St., telling the motel clerk he planned to stay for a week or 10 days.

BROUGHT SUITCASES

He had two suitcases and several shoe boxes with him, the clerk told police, and he put them into his room before leaving.

He apparently went from there to the St. Mary's Society Club, 1321 S. Main St., where he had two or three drinks and talked to bartender Anthony Schiro and several patrons.

He called a Rockford woman from the club, telling her he planned to stop at the home of his parents, Mr. and Mrs. Joseph LaFranka, 719 Cunningham St., to pick up some spaghetti sauce, and that he would come to her apartment for dinner.

LEFT CLUB

He left the club about 2 p.m.

No one has reported seeing LaFranka between that time and Saturday morning, nearly a week later, when his body was discovered in Elgin.

Rockford police hinted that LaFranka was involved in underworld activities in Chicago, where he had been living for the past several years, except for periodic visits to Rockford.

Detectives said LaFranka may have been picked up by Chicago hoodlums after he left the club and strangled in Rockford or during the ride to Elgin.

CHEESE FOUND

When the body was found, it was dressed in the same clothing LaFranka had been wearing when he left the club.

Also found in the car was a package of cheese, which a close relative said had probably been bought in Chicago as a gift for his mother.

Police said LaFranka had been in Rockford on Christmas Eve, and had quite a bit of money with him at the time, although he had been in debt when he left Rockford for Chicago four months before.

In 1959, while in Rockford, LaFranka had been questioned by sheriff's deputies in connection with the finding of the bodies of two men who had also been strangled to death and stuffed in the trunk of a car owned by one of them.

BODIES FOUND

Bodies of Joseph Patrick Greco Jr., 21, 615 Monatgue Road, and Donald L. Burton 21, also of Rockford, were discovered early in the morning of May 2, 1959, in the trunk of Greco's car. The car was parked on Montague Road, just east of Meridian Road.

Also found in Greco's car was a case containing several hundred pairs of dice.

The double-slaying has never been solved.

Slain Man Planned Sunday Dinner———

Woman Waited for Murder Victim

By RON LEYS
Morning Star Staff Writer

DONNA OTT DESCRIBED CHARLES LAFRANKA MONDAY NIGHT as "the finest man I've ever known."

Although LaFranka's body was found in the trunk of his car in Elgin last Saturday and evidence indicates he was strangled to death on the previous Sunday or Monday, she said she "never saw him go anywhere where everyone didn't like him."

Miss Ott said she had known LaFranka for years, and had been going with him for two years.

She said her 4-year-old daughter, Bonnie, "thought the world of him. I don't think he ever said a cross word to her. Kids seemed to like him."

LaFranka had a 4-year-old daughter of his own, and had stopped to visit his estranged wife and daughter, Tina, at their Oak Lawn home before coming to Rockford on the day he disappeared, Sunday, Jan. 10.

On that day LaFranka came to the St. Mary's Society Club, 1321 S. Main St., a place the couple often visited together. He called Miss Ott from there.

"I knew he was coming, so I bought a chicken on Saturday –– he loved fried chicken. He said he felt like spaghetti, and he said, 'We'll have spaghetti and chicken.'"

LaFranka was to cook the spaghetti and she would take care of the chicken.

He told her he was going to stop at his mother's home for some spaghetti sauce, and then would come to her place.

She started the chicken, but LaFranka didn't arrive.

She called his mother, and found he hadn't been there.

The last time he was seen alive was about 2 p. m. Sunday, when he left the club.

"It's been a nightmare since he's been gone. It's so hard to believe."

When he called her on what was probably the last day of his life, he was in an especially good mood, she said.

"I could tell that from his voice.

"Who would have thought that something like that could happen."

At this, her voice trailed off.

Banker Outlasts Bandit In Frantic, 2-State Chase

By RON LEYS
Morning Star Staff Writer

September 30, 1965

William A. Canary
. . . "This should teach them to stay out of Rock County"

Donald F. Retzlaff
. . . "I'm deadly serious"

ESIDES BEING A SUCCESSFUL BANK PRESIDENT, WILLIAM A. Canary, 68, of the Footville (Wis.) State Bank, proved to be an effective match for a gunman who robbed his bank late Wednesday morning.

After the robbery, Canary ran out of the bank, flagged down a passing car, and pursued the fleeing bandit over "all of Southern Wisconsin and Northern Illinois" before the robber's car ran out of gas and he fled into a cornfield near Harrison, Ill.

POSSE OF 60

A posse of about 60 officers from several law enforcement agencies surrounded the field and took Donald Retzlaff, 22, 1855 Wisconsin Ave., Beloit, Wis., into custody.

Canary said later, "This should teach them (bank robbers) to stay out of Rock County."

The whole story, as told by Canary, went like this:

Canary was in his office when he heard the bank's door open and shut. He went out to wait on the customer, and found instead a man carrying a pistol and holding a folded road map in front of his face.

PRACTICAL JOKE?

"I thought someone was pulling a practical joke, so I asked 'Are you serious?'"

"Yes, I'm deadly serious," the robber barked.

The gunman ordered Canary, his wife, Marie, and his son Paul, 26, into the bank's vault, and then approached clerk April Ronnenburg, 20, and told her to give him the bank's cash.

"What'll I put it in?" Miss Ronnenburg asked.

Canary told her to use one of the bank's paper bags. She filled a sack and pushed it over the counter to the robber.

The bandit told Canary to push a table in front of the open vault and then he turned and fled outside.

As soon as he left, Canary pushed the table aside and went into action.

He told his wife to call authorities and ran outside after the fleeing robber, who had gotten into a car and was driving north.

"I hollered at a car coming in the other direction to block the road, but he didn't understand," Canary said.

So the bank president stopped the car, driven by Maurice D. Bonaunet, 35, who owns a repair garage just north of Orfordville.

"I told him, 'That's a bank robber, let's chase him.' He said 'All right,' so we made a U-turn and were after him."

In the meantime, Canary's son Paul had jumped in his own car and was also in hot pursuit of the bandit's car. Bonaunet and the elder Canary fell into line and the chase was on.

After several miles of driving along county roads, the robber suddenly stopped and, at gunpoint, took Paul Canary's car keys. He had another set with him. When his father drew abreast of him the elder Canary shouted to his son to call authorities and tell them where they were.

By the time Paul Canary got back into his car to rejoin the chase, the other cars had disappeared.

His father recalled that he and Bonaunet drove through Hanover on County Trunk H, but "from there on, I don't know where we went.

"We must have covered all of Southern Wisconsin and Northern

Illinois. I remember going past the Wagon Wheel (a resort near Rockton, Ill.) three times."

SPEEDS, SLOWS DOWN

The chase sometimes reached speeds of 85 miles an hour and the pursued car dodged and twisted along country roads and highways, but most of the time the two autos traveled at between 60 and 70 miles an hour.

Several times the pursued can slowed to about 35 miles an hour.

Finally, on the second swing along Harrison Road, the robber's car apparently ran out of gas about three miles south of Harrison.

The bandit jumped from his car and ran into a cornfield. Bonaunet and Canary drove on by and stopped at the first farmhouse to call authorities and give their location.

Within minutes, squad cars began converging on the scene form all directions. The field was surrounded by about 60 officers, and Retzlaff surrendered soon afterward.

Canary gave the credit for the success of the chase to his driver, Bonaunet.

"He was quite a driver," the bank president said.

The River of Return

Up the creek without a paddle on . . .

May 16, 1984

Editor's Note: *When it comes to covering the really big stories, you don't send the cub reporters or the society columnists. You send the hardened, weathered professionals, the grim, tough veterans who can brush aside the insignificant and trivial, pierce through to the truth, and come back with The Really Big Story. This is one of those stories, written by one of those reporters. He has canoed the wildest rivers on the globe, survived for weeks alone in the wilderness, subsisting only on stale cigars, moose antler moss and pine cones, and when he stares into the face of danger, it is danger that blinks. This is his incredible story.*

By Ron Leys
Journal Outdoor Editor

GREAT AMERICA, ILLINOIS –– SOUTH, EVER SOUTH I PUSHED, heading for the wild country, hoping to shake the stink of civilization.

It was sometime after dawn when I crossed the border and hit the bumpy, poorly maintained roads that are a sure sign of an underdeveloped nation and people. I pulled up at a checkpoint called Waukegan Plaza, where hard-eyed border patrolmen were weighing trucks and, undoubtedly, collecting bribes from gringo drivers. I was waved through after a small payoff, and I resumed my journey south, always south.

Before long, the rolling hills of the Great America Range rose out of the monotonous plain, and I swung off the main road. It was still early, so I stopped for my standard wilderness breakfast: a sausage McMuffin with egg, chased with coffee, straight. There was work to be done, and not the kind of work you can do on cookies and milk.

Word had reached Milwaukee of a new river, cutting through the heart of the Great America Range, raging untamed and virtually unexplored. Journalists from throughout the country were to gather to conquer the river, soon nicknamed the White Water Rampage, and report back to their readers. I had been chosen by the Green Sheet editor to take the challenge.

Shortly after arrival, we gathered at the river and prepared to push off into the unknown. Lowering gray clouds spat rain and a chill wind added to the chill of fear; the usually talkative journalists fell silent as they peered over the cliff into the torrent below.

The waters were dirty brown, but foaming white where they were caught and compressed between unyielding stone cliffs; rapids pounded and roared in futile fury as the river fought to be free of its stone prison.

Kayakers from the Chicago Whitewater Association were first off, paddling furiously and then leaning hard on their double-bladed paddles in desperate efforts to remain upright. Journalists watched in dread as the kayakers were shot through three-foot-high standing waves, their boats disappearing and only the bodies of the brave men and women visible above the foam.

Then it was our turn. An outfitter had provided big, raft-like boats, round like Indian bull-boats and fitted with seats for a dozen or so persons.

I spurned company. The wilderness is best faced alone: one wilderness, one man.

But as I shoved off into a quiet eddy, I suddenly realized that the outfitter had forgotten to provide a paddle. Here I was, up a raging torrent without a paddle. Screams of other journalists who had gone ahead drifted down on the spray, foretelling my fate.

There was no turning back; the current was tugging at my raft and

I now belonged to the river. It could, and would, do to me whatever it wanted.

A bolt of terror shot through me, but I forced my hands to stop trembling and lit up a Dutch Master, hoping for a bit of Dutch courage. Bullets are fine to bite, but cigars taste better.

I could hear the roar of the beast now, and I clung grimly to the raft and chomped down hard on the cigar.

And now I was into it. The river swung around a bend and crashing, foaming waves clawed at the boat, trying to claim us, to smash us into debris and driftwood and broken bones.

The boat lurched and spun, bouncing now off cliff walls and now off obstacles in the water as the river roared and charged into an S turn. The raft shot out of the turn and suddenly the world went dark as the river churned through a cave.

There was just enough light reveal rows of tombstones in the cave, marking where others had not been so lucky as I.

Suddenly I was out of the cave and the boat rolled and plunged through series of stair-step standing waves, sudden splash and my cigar fizzled and went out, but I chomped even harder and hung on for my life.

And then it was over, as suddenly as it had begun. The raft bobbed gently in a quiet stretch as though nothing had ever happened, as though it and I had been up a lazy river on Sunday afternoon.

I accepted the handshakes of my colleagues. The White Water Rampage had been tamed.

We celebrated and laughed and shouted and pounded each other on the back. But it was over. And there was, as always, a lingering sadness. Another spot on the Earth's surface had yielded to the dominion of man.

I headed back to civilization, with one thought in mind: find a pretty girl and a glass of Canadian Club and be thankful to be alive to enjoy them.

Great America, with its new ride in the White Water Rampage, is open weekends through May 20.

—Journal Photos by Lynn Howell

Veteran outdoorsman and canoeist Ron Leys chomped down hard on his
cigar as his fragile little craft was pummeled and buffeted by the raging
torrents of a frightening, untamed waterway. It was man against the
elements, and the elements were sorry they ever showed up . . .

A honey Of A hobby

September 21, 1980

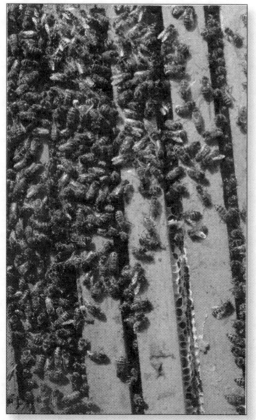

By Ron Leys of The Journal

BEEKEEPING, IT HAS BEEN SAID, IS A GENTLE CRAFT. AND SO IT is. The beekeepers I have met tend to be quiet, gentle people. Maybe that's because beekeeping, like gardening and fishing, appeals to people who like to do things by themselves, rather than with large groups — things that are practical and that have a point, a point that does not involve besting another, as in golf or tennis.

And perhaps it is because some people are drawn into beekeeping through a fascination with nature.

But maybe, just maybe, beekeepers are a gentle people because that is the kind of people bees like.

Dogs and cows respect someone who is firm and forceful; someone who will make them do things. But you can't make a bee do anything. And a bee will almost never sting someone who moves quietly and gently as he takes apart the hive to see what the bees might need this week.

Honeybees themselves are gentle and go about their business with remarkably little fuss, paying no attention to the people or dogs or cats around them.

We are talking now about honeybees. This does not necessarily apply to the wasps and hornets that also inhabit our world. Folks often think of them as bees, but of course they are not.

There are thousands upon thousands of honeybees in the two hives next to the sun porch at our home in the Milwaukee suburb of Bayside. These bees have never threatened anyone.

One of my favorite relaxations is to hunker down just to one side of a hive entrance on a warm, sunny day and watch the bees come and go.

The departing bees come out onto the landing board at the bottom of the hive and are into the air in the same motion. They fly straight off. In a beeline, you might say.

The arriving bees land every second or so and head immediately into the darkness of the hive. They don't even glance my way.

Some carry drops of golden nectar inside their bodies. On others, the baskets on their back legs bulge with pollen. Some pollen is red, some is gray, some bright yellow. On a given day, however, the bees tend to return with the same color pollen.

There's a reason for that. But before we get into it, let's explain that bees are not really kept. They keep themselves. They make almost all of the decisions. They run the hive. And, unlike sheep or horses, they are free to come and go as they please. If they all decide to leave one day, they do.

My beekeeping partner is my son, Tony. Our main job is to set up a comfortable, safe home. We make our own hive boxes, taking pains to leave three-eighths of an inch around every part inside.

A Lutheran minister in Pennsylvania discovered in 1851 that if he left three-eighths of an inch around the honeycomb frames in his backyard hive, the bees would use the space as passageways and would refrain from gluing everything in the hive together into a huge mass, as they normally do.

The beekeeper then can take the hive apart in the fall and remove some of the bees' winter stores for himself. The rest he can leave for the bees.

Tony and I bought knocked-down frames, which when nailed together look something like picture frames. Into those we fastened flat sheets of wax that are embossed with the hexagonal pattern of bee cells. The bees build their nursery and storage cells on this foundation.

We hang 10 of these frames vertically in each hive box, and the bees do the rest. The only thing we so-called beekeepers do is open the hive once every week or so and make sure the bees still have enough room to raise their young and store their food. As we work, we puff smoke into the hive, which calms the bees.

If are running short of space, we add another story — called a super — to the home.

Tony and I started out this spring with one colony left from last year's operation and one new hive. We sent a check off to the York Bee Co., a bee-breeding farm in Jesup, Ga.

The bees arrived one day by mail — in a wood and screen box with stamps on the top. The guys in the post office weren't too nuts about the whole idea and asked me to pick them up.

I explained that I couldn't. I had my own job to go to. So the mailman delivered those thousands of unhappy, buzzing bees.

LATER that day Tony and I opened the box and dumped the bees into the empty hive. We put a cover on the hive, but left the entrance open on the bottom. All we could do was hope they liked their new home and would decide to stay. To our relief, they did. Sometimes bees do not.

Our other hive had survived the winter, although the colony was down to a couple of thousand bees.

We knew that the queen was supposed to start laying eggs heavily early in the spring, building up the number of bees so the colony could take full advantage of the millions of fruit tree blossoms that would pop all at once.

Yes, millions. A policeman friend who knows about bees told me that bees must visit 2½ million clover blossoms to make a pound of clover honey. And a hive of bees will make several hundred pounds of honey in a year.

But we noticed that this queen didn't seem to be laying eggs like she should.

I was all for ordering a new queen from Georgia, but Tony suggested that we wait a bit.

While we procrastinated, the bees acted.

Like the queens of Britain and the Netherlands, queen bees reign only at the sufferance of their subjects.

One day, apparently a committee meeting was held. A worker bee made a motion to create a new queen, someone seconded and the motion was passed.

The workers now made a new kind of cell. It was several times bigger than a normal cell and looked like a peanut in size and shape.

The queen dutifully laid a fertilized female egg in the cell. If told to by the workers, the queen also can lay an unfertilized male egg that will become a drone. But that is another story.

As soon as the egg in the queen cell hatched into a tiny larva, the workers began feeding it around the clock with a rich substance that beekeepers call royal jelly.

Because of the special diet –– ordinary larvae are served a mixture of honey and pollen and become non-reproducing workers –– the specially-selected larva developed full reproductive organs and went into hibernation.

When she emerged, she was a queen. She immediately went looking for the old queen, and killed her.

Murdered her, you say? Well, that is your word. It must be kept in mind that honeybees and humans are social animals, and as such, share many habits and tendencies. But that similarity does not make them identical.

So now there was one queen again. A virgin queen, you might say. But she didn't stay that way for long.

She took off on her honeymoon flight, and several of the drones that hang around hive entrances took off after her.

One caught up with her, mated with her in the air and fell dead.

The queen returned and entered the hive, never to leave again —— unless the whole colony tells her they are leaving. Then she probably will go along.

When Tony and I checked the hive a couple of weeks later, we could see that the new queen was doing fine. The hive was almost boiling over with bees, and comb after comb were filled with the new brood.

NOW BACK to that business about all the bees carrying the same color pollen. Here's why.

You can believe this or not, as you choose, but the man who discovered and explained it in the 1920s finally got a Nobel Prize for his work in 1973. And scientist after scientist —— bees are studied a lot because of their economic importance —— have confirmed this.

The first bees to leave the hives in the early morning are scout bees. Their job is to find a huge number of identical flowers blooming within a mile or so of the hive.

The flowers must be identical because bees are programmed by their instincts to go only to one kind of lower on any given collecting trip.

That is for the immediate benefit of the flower, and the long-range benefit of the bee. The plant, you see, grows a flower only to attract a bee. It wants the bee to crawl down inside after the drop of nectar and grains of pollen. The drop of nectar is there for the immediate benefit of the bee, and the long-range benefit of the flower.

That's because as the bee crawls in to get the nectar, or to fill its pollen baskets, some pollen sticks to its body.

When the bee goes to the next flower –– which is shaped and colored and perfumed so it is distinct from flowers of other species –– some of the pollen accidentally is brushed onto the female organs of the flower, and sexual reproduction can begin. Next year there will be new flowers to nourish new bees.

So the scout bee looks for a mass of identical flowers that thousands of bees can use to make several pounds of honey in a day. She ignores those four tulips by your back door and heads for the flowering crab apple tree in your neighbor's yard.

When she returns to her hive, other bees gather around. She passes out samples of the sweet nectar she has found.

Then she does a dance. If the nectar source is within 300 yards of the hive, she dances about in a circle, taking quick, short steps. She may do this in several places in the hive, each time gathering an excited audience.

Then she runs to the entrance, and takes off. The other bees follow, one by one.

BUT if the flower source is farther from the hive, things get more complicated.

In that case the scout waggles her backside as she dances, and steps about in various patterns, perhaps a series of half-circles, perhaps in a crescent pattern. At some point, she will make a straight run as she repeats this pattern.

As she dances, she sings.

From her song and from the pattern and from the number of times she runs in a straight line, the scout tells the other bees how far off the flower are.

The scout's body has picked up some of the aromatic oils manufactured by the flowers. The bees in the audience smell this and use it to help home in on the flowers.

Some researchers believe that the scout also tells her fellow workers what color to look for. Bees can see rather well, and in color. That is why roses are red and violets are blue. It isn't for us and our silly poems.

But the scout's most important information is the direction of the flower source. After all, if the flowers are a mile or so away, the other bees can't see or smell them as they leave the hive.

So the bees watch the straight line taken across a vertical honey comb.

Opening a hive — Toney Leys puffs smoke into a hive from a metal firepot device (right) while his dad lifts off a story — called a super. The smoke calms worker bees, which cluster atop frames (left). The stingless drone above is tame as a kitten as it clings to a bit of wood held by a gloved hand.

Photography by John Biever of The Journal

Tony and Ron Lys and one of their combs, covered with bees. If a closer look is needed, the bees can be moved gently out of the way with the brush.

Wild River in Our Back Yard

By RON LEYS
of The Journal Staff

A river willow shades the canoe below the Newburg Dam.

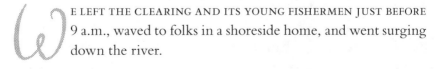

E LEFT THE CLEARING AND ITS YOUNG FISHERMEN JUST BEFORE 9 a.m., waved to folks in a shoreside home, and went surging down the river.

These were the last people we were to see for three hours as our canoe and the current carried us through a seemingly endless forest. There were no bridges, no fishermen, no riverside cottages, no resorts, no contact with the civilization we were leaving behind.

Birds flitted through the huge willows, oaks and maples as we rounded bend after bend on the swift current. Their songs were constantly in the air, even on this hot and humid day. Half-grown ducks floundered and flapped in panic ahead of us, wishing they could fly away from the alien invaders.

=============

Paddle Power

=============

Paddling was almost unnecessary, except to steer now and then, and there was time to talk and philosophize on this languid voyage.

As we discussed the latest adventures of Zonker Harris, our Doonesbury hero, a deer appeared in brush along the shore. Seemingly unaccustomed to man, it moved only a few feet as I maneuvered the canoe so my son Jon, paddling bow, could get a look. He did, as the deer sauntered back into the forest.

The river was the Milwaukee, and we had launched our canoe just below the dam at the east end of West Bend, well within what is often referred to as the Milwaukee metropolitan area. The dam is behind a machine shop along Highway 33.

As a prophet is without honor within 30 miles of home, so is a river. The Milwaukee River is much maligned, and deserves some of its reputation. But in its upper reaches, the river is clean enough to support an abundance of fish. I recall casting spoons to a cut bank near Kewaskum and the northern pike that stormed out to slash at them.

However, below West Bend, there are problems. Although we did not fish on the day of our recent trip, there were clues to tell us that our chances of success would have been small.

We saw not a single heron all day. Normally, one surprises a great blue heron every couple of miles on a river trip. Little green herons and night herons are not uncommon sights along Wisconsin rivers, but we saw none. We did see a few kingfishers, but only at mill ponds behind dams.

Mill pond dams were also the only places where we saw people fishing, and those people were all under the age of 12.

These dams, by the way, are the only real hazard in the rivers in southeast Wisconsin when water levels are normal or slightly above. (In flood stages, as in recent days, any river can become dangerous and should be approached with caution, if at all.)

From downstream, the dams are obvious, each one looking like a miniature Niagara Falls. But canoes don't travel that way, at least not canoes I travel in. Since they ride with the current, they approach dams from upstream. From this vantage, a dam is not nearly as obvious.

ONE SHOULD be on the lookout for dams at all times and be ready to portage around them. Some are only two feet high, others are much higher. But, I would not try to run any of them. Even a low dam will often have a backroller wave at the bottom that will tumble a canoe and a pool of turbulent water that will keep him from swimming free.

So how do you tell where there is a dam?

The first sign usually is a cessation of current. You become aware that you have been paddling harder. As the current slows, water lilies find secure holding areas and their pads are seen on the surface. The water gets deeper; paddles are no longer touching bottom. The river has gone from maybe two feet deep to five feet. And it is obviously wider.

Roads, houses, churches and schools will appear along the shore. The dam was originally erected to power a mill —— usually a grist mill to grind the wheat that was once grown here. A town grew up around the mill. Most of the mills are now gone, but the settlements remain.

Stick to the shoreline and watch carefully. Suddenly you notice that there is something odd about the scenery ahead. It looks like a picture that has had a piece cut out of the middle, and the top has been glued back to the bottom.

Sometimes there will be a bridge over the dam. This is the case at Newburg, the first settlement we hit the other day. We pulled up at the cemetery on the right bank at 1 p.m., spent a few minutes reading the

19th century tombstones, and walked up for a sandwich and cold pop at Duey's Bar.

FOR OUTLANDERS who might not be familiar with Wisconsin crossroad settlements, there is usually no restaurant in town. But since the farmers who come in on errands get hungry, one or another of the several taverns in each settlement will usually be serving sandwiches. And often pizza.

We left Duey's, browsed in an antique store, then carried the canoe over the road and dam and were back on the river.

I told Jon that the River-edge Nature Center was somewhere in the area, and his response was: "How could you tell? This is all a nature center."

And so it is.

As 5 p.m. approached, we sensed that we were in another mill pond, and soon a big feed mill reared up on the right bank. Waubeka.

The mill marks the dam at Waubeka. The main street carries Highway 84 over the river a block downstream, so the bridge is not at the dam. The only place we found to take our canoe out was just above the mill.

JON AND I headed for the Village Inn, where we dined on Tombstone pizza and shot pool while waiting for mother and wife Marilyn to come and collect us.

Later, as we drove along the heights above the river valley, we could see clearly that the wilderness we thought we had been canoeing through was only a narrow strip, winding through the countryside. When the land was cleared many years ago, the brush and willows were left, probably because the willows were of such little value for lumber.

That has provided the teeming throngs of the Milwaukee area with corridors of scenic and wild beauty in which to spend a day off in the summertime. But very few do. In my half dozen or so trips down various stretches of the Milwaukee River, the number of other canoeists I have run into could be counted on my fingers.

It only costs a couple of bucks to rent a canoe –– look under Boats-Rental in the Yellow Pages. Instructions are offered at low fees by such groups as the Red Cross, the YMCA and the Wisconsin Canoe Association.

The only equipment necessary is life saver (and fanny saver) cushions, life preservers, a canteen of water, a couple of balogna sandwiches, insect repellent, a hat, a raincoat and a sense of adventure.

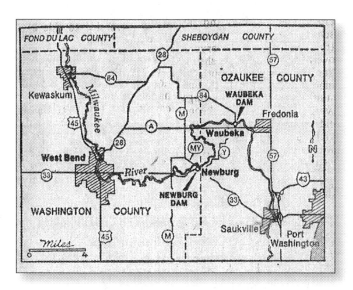

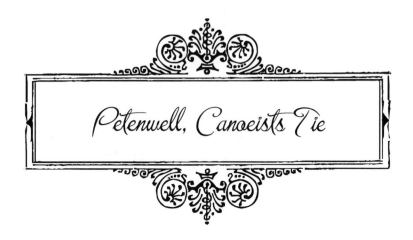

Petenwell, Canoeists Tie

June 10, 1979

Discover writer Ron Leys is completing the third week of his canoe trip down the Wisconsin River from the Michigan border to the Iowa line with a series of partners. This week he reports on the trip from Knowlton, north of Stevens Point, to Wisconsin Dells.

By RON LEYS
of The Journal Staff

ISCONSIN DELLS, WIS. -- PETENWELL. WE ROUNDED AN island downstream from Nekoosa, and there it was. So vast we couldn't see the far shore.

The sun was sparkling off the waves and the wind was blowing. Right in our faces.

When we started making plans last winter to canoe the 400-plus mile length of the Wisconsin River, people whose outdoor experience is limited to parades, picnics and ballgames said they hoped it wouldn't rain.

But the people who know something about the rivers and lakes of Wisconsin didn't mention rain. They, like us, accept rain as part of the natural order of things and are not greatly bothered by it.

What they did is ask a question. Always the same one: "What will you do if you run into headwinds on the Petenwell Flowage?"

The only answer I could give was that we would lay over until the wind turned or died.

That would bring a knowing smile. Sure. Maybe you guys should hire somebody to truck you around Petenwell, and the Castle Rock Flowage below it. Maybe you should take an outboard. Maybe you don't realize how bad that lake gets.

"Well, this is it," I said to Russ Kramer in the bow. "Let's try for that point."

Petenwell's west shore is a series of points, as if someone had cut the coast out with a giant pinking shears. The nearest headland was about two miles off and offered just a little protection from the stiff breeze.

"Okay," Russ said gamely.

The waves were about a foot high. Nothing at all for a good sized runabout or sailboat, but something else for a loaded canoe with about six inches of freeboard along the sides.

We strained against the paddles, struggling to move the heavy craft. It would stop dead after each stroke, leaving no momentum to help on the next.

The bow rose slowly, almost drunkenly, to each big wave, then fell with a metallic thunk into the trough behind.

AFTER ABOUT a half hour, I shouted: "We can't make it; let's try for that island ahead."

An eternity later, we came into the lee of the arrowhead shaped island, but its shores were brushy and impenetrable from the water.

The nearby mainland was worse. Thirty foot high banks of crumbling, yellow sand.

So we spent the evening and night camped on a marshy, sandy spit at one end of the island, a scant six inches above the water.

I predicted confidently that the wind would drop that night and we could put on many miles if we started early the next morning, before the wind made up again in the afternoon.

But the wind howled through the runty willows all night. It still was blowing hard as we spooned down oatmeal in the morning. We started out, however, hugging the shoreline and going from point to point.

Until we came to Long View Point. The shore behind it falls away to the west, giving us no protection from the south wind that was sweeping up two foot waves across 15 miles of open water.

Still, we tried. Solid water spilled into the boat. Then, we gave up. We put our tails between our legs and ran for shore, scooting back around the point for safety.

BLACK CLOUDS appeared in the west and after about two hours rain began to spatter down on our landing place. But the wind died when the rains began.

Off we went. Still hugging the shore, but now for the sake of safety in case a thunderstorm roared in.

We spent the rest of the day paddling against moderate headwinds and looking nervously over our shoulders as rain fell softly and thunder began to mutter.

By late afternoon, the thunder was booming from a storm just to our right and sheets of rain were hanging down to our left as we ghosted in a flat calm towards the dam at the bottom of the Petenwell.

DEAD TIRED. But exultant.

"I never thought we'd see this dam today," I said.

"Me either," Russ said with a happy grin.

We portaged around the dam and made camp in Mosquito City. There was a backwater swamp behind our camp, and we were the answer to the prayers of the millions of mosquitos who had been born there.

We choked down beef stew and bread and dove for our tents.

The next day dawned bright and sunny, and after a big breakfast of hash and eggs we were off for the Castle Rock Flowage.

We hit it lucky. Winds blew off the eastern shore for the 12 mile length of the flowage, so we hugged that shore and by 2 o'clock we were at the dam.

We had even taken time to talk to a Department of Natural Resources crew that was checking a fyke net as part of a study of the lake's fish.

"This is an excellent lake," said Joe Keena, a fish management technician as he pulled big crappies and medium sized walleyes from the net. "But it's very under-fished."

HE TALKED as he worked, clipping tags on fins and calling out measurements to Ian Chisholm, a DNR intern and University of Wisconsin — Stevens Point student. With them was Mark Kaisersatt from a co-operative state and

—*By a Journal Artist*
*The Discover expedition canoed from Knowlton
to Wisconsin Dells in the past week.*

federal civil works program, the Young Adult Conservation Corps.

"I don't believe there is a walleye run anywhere that's better than the one at the Nekoosa Dam," Keena said. "Yes, I'm including the Wolf River run. And there's a white bass run going on now that's also better than the one on the Wolf. Fishermen are coming off with baskets full."

He acknowledged that the Wisconsin River and its central Wisconsin flowages had an image problem. Like bad tasting fish. Like fish that were once so contaminated that the DNR told people flatly not to eat them.

But those days are over, Keena said.

"I've been eating fish out of these flowages for two years, and they taste good," he said.

I immediately thought of all the spanking new waste disposal plants noted by me and my previous partners, first Don Bluhm, who paddled 130 miles with me from the source of the river to Merrill, and then Pat Reardon, who took the 100 miles down to Nekoosa.

A Consolidated Paper Co. facility below Stevens Point, where Pat and I had portaged wearily around three dams in a row, was labeled "Water Renewal Center."

GEORGE Wotruba, who lives along the river north of Wisconsin Rapids, had talked enthusiastically about how the river had changed from a smelly murk in which "you couldn't see your hand four inches under the water."

"Now you can walk out in three feet of water and see your feet," he said.

He also talked about how fishing had improved.

Was it worth all the money and effort? I asked.

He gave me the look people reserve for reporters who ask very dumb questions, and after a minute or so said: "It would've gotten like the rivers in Chicago in a few years."

An old fisherman in Stevens Point who called the Wisconsin "the finest river in the world" had said its waters looked like a chocolate malt five or six years ago and its fish were not edible then.

He added, however, that because the problem had gotten so bad, with mills and cities dumping sewage and chemicals into the river for 100 years, it would be a while longer before the organisms that give life to a river would completely recover.

The mills do appear to be trying to be good neighbors these days.

When Pat and I had seen the raging torrent and mile long portage below the big Consolidated mill in Wisconsin Rapids, we decided to cheat and take a previous Consolidated offer to truck us around.

THE CREW that came for us hauled us all the way to Nekoosa, around the stairstep of dams in the stretch where the Wisconsin River tumbles down from the Northern Highlands into the state's Central Plains.

At Nekoosa, Pat had left for his home in Shorewood and Russ joined me after driving up from Sheboygan.

After making it through the Petenwell and Castle Rock Flowages, Russ and I found ourselves camped in a meadow about 10 miles north of Wisconsin Dells.

I sat on the bank that evening, watching the river roll freely along at my feet. A motto of the Wisconsin Valley Improvement Co., which plays an important role in wringing electricity from the Wisconsin River, came to mind: "One less river to boss."

The electricity and the water needed in the process of making paper no doubt are a big factor in the prosperity of the Wisconsin River Valley.

We came through The Dells the next morning, dodging powerful tourist cruise boats and the dangerous wake some of them raised as the river is squeezed between cliffs barely 50 feet apart.

We're headed for the last of 26 dams, at Prairie du Sac. From there to the Mississippi, no one has tried to boss the Wisconsin River.

That's the part of the river I love best.

*ASSISTED BY Bill McGinley (left) from the Nekoosa paper mill,
Ron Leys (center) and Russ Kramer haul their canoe to a truck as
they begin the portage around a Wisconsin River dam.*

— Journal Photos by Sherman A. Gessert Jr.

Montana: A Wild and Wonderful Escape

By Ron Leys
Journal Outdoor Editor

October 14, 1984

—— Bill Van Pietersom Photos

*The vast Bob Marshall Wilderness is off limits to motorized
vehicles, but not to man on foot or horseback*

HE GREAT MONTANA ELK HUNT ENDED LIKE THIS:

Three Wisconsin hunters limped and shuffled across a big parking lot toward a restaurant in western Minnesota.

Bill Van Pietersom was swinging his right leg out in front because his knee had popped out of place when the leg caught between two windfall logs on a steep mountainside.

Ken Hollnagel was walking with kind of a step and a half, favoring the ankle with a tendon torn when he tripped over a tent support in the pitch dark.

I was hunched over to the left, trying to hold back the pain from a rib that had snapped when a horse fell on me in the middle of a mountain stream.

Suddenly Bill laughed and said: "If they ask us what we do, tell them we get drunk. And we get in fights."

We all roared with laughter, even though it brought such pain in my side that tears came to my eyes.

The meat trailer we had towed all the way to western Montana was just as empty as when we left home.

We had each paid $1,800 to get snowed on, half-frozen, roused from our tents in the middle of the night, scared half to death at nearly perpendicular slopes traversed on foot and on horseback, and led back to our tent camp long after dark, too tired to even talk. On top of it all, we had been turned into a ragged band of cripples.

And it had been worth every penny.

We had heard the high, wild, whistling bugle of a bull elk at dawn, answering the challenge sent out by a first-class hunting guide.

We had seen proud bulls, heads held high to show off their enormous spreads of antlers, far off on snowy mountainsides. I had watched in wonder as a half-grown elk, already bigger than a Wisconsin deer, knelt to nurse at its mother, just 40 yards from me and a guide. We had gasped in awe from mountain peaks as we looked out over range after range of snowy mountains. We had gaped as we rode through forests of 80- and 100-foot trees. We had eaten like kings, dining each day on food served up by one of the best cooks I have ever known.

It was an experience that will never be forgotten, one that will be told and retold in walleye boats, duck blinds and deer hunting camps for years to come.

Unspoiled, Untouched by Man

Ron Leys

Journal Outdoor Editor

Ron Leys stood at the doorway to the wilderness

ILDERNESS, ACCORDING TO THE UNITED STATES GOVERNMENT, is a place where man is but a visitor.

Wilderness, according to the New York City-born man for whom the Bob Marshall Wilderness of Montana is named, is a "region sufficiently spacious that a person may spend at least a week or two of travel ... without crossing his own tracks."

Wilderness, to this city boy, is a place where we can see the world as it really is, as all of it was before the cancer known as civilization began to infect almost every corner of the earth.

It's a place where, as Jesus and John the Baptist and Elijah once did, we can go to get back in touch with the values that really count, the values of nature.

I have wandered like a nomad across several federally protected wildernesses –– by canoe in the Boundary Waters of Minnesota, with a backpack in the Selway-Bitterroot of Idaho.

Came to hunt

But this time, I came to the wilderness as a predator, an elk hunter, armed with a rifle as the grizzly bear that inhabits these mountains is armed with claws and teeth and as the eagle seen here is armed with talons and beak.

The outfitters and guides we lived with in our tent camp have a love-hate relationship with the Bob Marshall Wilderness –– advertising it, selling it and professing to love the wildness of it, but cursing Eastern environmentalists, the government and especially the US Forest Service, which has the job of keeping the wilderness a wilderness.

Wildernesses don't just happen, not in this country. They are normally areas that are so wild, so remote, that other parts of the country were raped first.

By the time the mining companies, the timber barons, the oil companies, the developers got to eyeing the few beauties that were left, the public had become aware enough, and the government had gotten strong enough, to say no.

"Unspoiled wilderness"

After a hunting trip in northern Mexico during the late 1930s, Aldo Leopold said:

"It was here that I first clearly realized that land is an organism, that all my life I had seen only sick land, whereas here was a biota still in perfect aboriginal health. The term 'unspoiled wilderness' took on a new meaning."

Indeed, it is no accident that the Americans who taught us the value of wilderness were from the East and Midwest, from areas where the well had gone dry and the water was missed.

Some of the names that come immediately to mind are Leopold of Wisconsin, Henry Thoreau of Connecticut, Gifford Pinchot of Pennsylvania, Sigurd Olson of Minnesota and Robert Marshall of New York City.

Marshall, who earned degrees from the New York State College of Forestry, Harvard University and Johns Hopkins University, learned about the wilderness in upstate New York and then in Montana and Idaho.

From his teens, he hiked the trails of the wild areas, often 50 miles in a day, sometimes 70 miles.

Took his name

Marshall became so well known as a wilderness advocate that the Roosevelt Administration chose him to write the forest recreation part of a National Plan for American Forestry, submitted to Congress in 1933.

In his paper, Marshall recommended the setting aside of 45 million acres, including roadside parks, campgrounds, national parks and 10 million acres of wilderness. Much of his plan was eventually adopted.

In 1941, two years after his death of a heart attack at the age of 38, the western Montana wilderness was named for Bob Marshall.

And so it is because of this son of a wealthy Jewish family that my friends and I were able to enter a world whose door is a long and difficult trail usable only by human or horse or mule feet.

Lovely Place

November 21, 1982

—— Journal Photo by Ron Leys

A rear view of Ron Leys' log cabin, which overlooks the peaceful
setting of Crow Hollow in Crawford County

Home away from home is surrounded by friends

Back Yard, Back Country
By Ron Leys
Journal Outdoor Editor

OUNT ZION, WIS. –– IT'S ONLY A CABIN . . .

It's certainly not a cottage. For one thing, there's no lake lapping softly 100 feet away. For another, there's no plumbing. Just a hand pump down the hill and an outhouse up the hill. No electric lights, no television, no toaster.

It's not a country home. It's only got one room, after all.

It's not even a wilderness retreat. Not really. Although there is a patch of woods to the west, you couldn't call our place a forest hideaway. Corn grew last summer in a field right behind the cabin, and barns and farmhouses are prominent on the ridge across the valley.

In the morning, you can hear a rooster crow and a farmer curse his cows.

Aware of neighbors

At 7:30 every weekday morning, the school bus mutters its way down the gravel road that hugs the hillside as it cuts across our 40 acres. A little later, the milk truck chugs its way up the road.

We are, if anything, more aware of our neighbors here in Crawford County than we are back in Milwaukee County.

The front of the cabin is almost six feet off the ground, with a door opening to nowhere because we might build a deck some day. The front wall of the cabin is high, simply because we found it easier to build a shed-type roof, with only one slope.

The rear doorsill is one step up from ground level — you step through the back door and you're inside.

The first thing you notice is three log posts that hold up the main beam.

That beam is actually two massive 3 by 12 white pine timbers that once held up a Milwaukee factory or warehouse floor; now they bear the center of the roof, plus whatever weight of snow winter lays on it.

Vivid memory

The memory of raising that main beam is a vivid one: teenage sons Tony and Jon, plus a friend, Mike Himmelfarb, and the bull of the woods, grunting and straining as they lifted one end at a time, a few feet at a time, going up in stages until the beams rested in notches in the end walls and met in the center, the joint hidden by one of the log posts.

The roof above is covered with asphalt roll roofing that Jon and I tarred down on a day when it was 100 degrees on the ground and at least 10 degrees hotter than that on the roof.

Jon will never forget that day, and neither will I. But the roof doesn't leak a drop. I think of Jon, now far away at an Army base in Colorado, every time a summer thunderstorm drums on the roof. You done good, kid.

The floor is only cheap No. 2 pine, tongued and grooved at a Milwaukee lumberyard.

Not a toolshed

But it's sound and tight. When Tony was sweating to force two warped boards together before nailing them, I remarked that it was only a cabin.

He looked up and said, "Maybe, but it's not a toolshed."

The windows that overlook our little valley are double casements that we got for the right price.

Wife Marilyn was taking a walk one evening near our Milwaukee County home when she saw eight sets of windows leaning against a tree in a front yard.

She asked the foreman of the remodeling crew what he planned to do with the windows.

"Haul 'em to the dump," was the reply.

We hauled them instead, in our pickup truck. And now we look out through them.

Making friends

The high front wall helped us meet some of our neighbors. We ran out of logs, and the front wall is a 2 by 6 frame, covered on the outside with rough-sawn pine clapboards.

We built the frame on the floor, then found we could not lift it into place. In desperation, I walked down the valley until I found a man home. I introduced myself and explained our plight.

An hour later, three men, three women, two dogs, a cake, a watermelon and a bouquet of wildflowers arrived.

We raised the wall and I went to the nearest tavern for a case of beer, and now we're all friends.

The cooking range is my mother's old gas stove. I rescued it from the basement after Dad died and Mom sold the house. I put new jets in the cast-iron stove to convert it to LP gas, and the first time I opened the oven after it was installed, I almost cried. The squeal of protest was the same sound I had heard as a little boy every time Mom opened the oven, which was pretty often, let me tell you.

Crooked chimney

The chimney is just a bit crooked. A neighboring farmer had stopped by as I was building it, and as we talked about alfalfa and cows I didn't notice that the blocks weren't going up exactly straight.

But it draws perfectly, and I can hear the wood popping in the stove as I write this on a cold, snowy night.

The table I'm writing on was given to us by my aunt, Emma Leys. The table and its chairs had been given to her and Uncle Peter as a wedding present by my grandfather.

After Uncle Pete died, Aunt Em sold their house. She gave us the kitchen set, saying that it should stay in the family and not be sold to strangers at a rummage sale.

Aunt Em and Uncle Pete had only each other, and no children ever used the chairs as a jungle gym or as sawhorses. They're perfect still.

Aunt Em is gone now too, but we think of her when we sit down to dinner here.

Bunks in the corner

The bunk beds in the corner were a winter project. Building them was a way of enjoying the cabin when we couldn't get out to it.

The kitchen cabinets came from the home of a good friend who thought of us as he was remodeling his home.

We sometimes drive up here as a family. Other times a gang of men fill the cabin with cigar smoke and laughter in between fishing or duck hunting on the Mississippi 15 miles away.

But I came up here alone on this weekend, as I often do. I just finished the dishes after my standard cabin supper –– steak, fried potatoes, canned mushrooms, corn and a bottle of beer.

I just lit a cigar and opened another beer.

Don't you get lonely up there, friends often ask.

Lonely? How could I get lonely, when I'm surrounded by friends.

It's only a cabin . . .

Friend or Foe? It's Not Always So Simple

March 1, 1981

BACK YARD BACK COUNTRY

By RON LEYS, of The Journal Staff

AST SUMMER, FRIENDS COMPLAINED THAT BEES HAD INVADED their yards and were making life impossible.

At the same time, my wife was remarking that her life was easier because the cauliflower and broccoli and cabbage that we grow in the garden had none of the usual green worms in them, and the apples were cleaner than usual.

The unhappiness and the happiness had a common cause.

The winter of 1979-'80, you will recall, was one of the mildest in years. Most humans who live in Wisconsin were delighted, especially since that winter had followed two back-to-back winters of towering snowdrifts and endless weeks of bitter cold.

As it turned out, we were not the only creatures that found life a little easier during that balmy winter.

Unseen by us, thousands of yellowjacket wasp queens and many bald-faced hornet queens had crawled away into cracks in trees and barns and stone walls around the state. Each queen was alone.

The first blast of cold weather had killed the colonies of hornets in their hanging paper nests and yellowjackets in their paper-lined holes in the ground. But by then the queens had left to keep the genetic fires burning.

In a normal year, winter would find and kill most of those hidden queens, while leaving enough to keep yellowjackets and hornets going as species the next summer.

But in that mild winter, most of the queens survived, and last summer they established colonies in back yards from one end of the state to the other.

That's why you thought you had so many bees in your yard last July. They were not bees at all, but there is good reason why you should think they were.

Bees and wasps are closely related, and most of them are boldly striped, usually black and yellow, but often black and white. That is a warning. It's a warning to us that the insect carries a sac of poison and a needle with which to inject that poison under our skins. And that hurts.

MY SON TONY and I are amateur beekeepers. As such, we get stung from time to time. We have built up a little immunity, and our arms and legs no longer swell and throb for hours after we are stung. But when that stinger goes into me, it feels like someone has hit me, hard, with a leather strap. If a bee gets me in the fanny as I am bending down to steal the honey she worked all summer to store, I straighten up real fast.

But the bee or wasp has a way of signaling first, just as a rattlesnake does. Because, even with a stinger, that bee or wasp is pretty small and stands a good chance of being killed in a fight with a bigger animal. So it prefers to flash its danger signal at us.

And from the dread with which bees and wasps are regarded by humans who have not had much experience with them, we can infer that our brain-computers are programed from birth to recognize that striped flag, and to avoid it.

We don't have to be taught to be afraid of bees and wasps, any more than we have to be taught to be afraid of snakes, although teaching may reinforce and strengthen the instinctive dread in both cases. We rather have to be taught, or have to teach ourselves, that bees and wasps have a rightful and valuable place in this world we all share, and that they will not hurt us if we leave them alone.

And we also have to learn that even if they do hurt us, they will not kill us, and we needn't reorder our whole lives or cover the world with our own brands of poison just in order to avoid being stung.

There is an exception, of course, and that is the person who has a severe allergy to bee and wasp venom. I'm not talking about the person whose arm swells up and throbs when stung by a couple of jellowjackets. That's a normal reaction, and Lord knows it's happened to me a time or two.

I'm talking about the person who is in danger of stopping breathing if stung. He or she usually has had a warning — an episode that involved

Bald-faced hornet

**—Sketches by Journal artist
Mario D. Cain**

a severe and frightening reaction. The next reaction could be the last one. That person shouldn't get advice from scribblers like me, he or she should get advice and perhaps desensitizing treatments from a doctor.

But most of us are not in that category, so we can all calm down after our initial panic on seeing a wasp or bee.

ONE MORE THING: What's the difference between a hornet and a wasp and a bee? A hornet is a kind of wasp, usually quite a big one. Our common bald-faced hornet is black and white on both its abdomen and head and is about three-quarters of an inch long. A yellowjacket is a smaller wasp, about a half inch, with a bright yellow and black body and head.

Most wasps are shiny, while most bees are fuzzy. Bees have fuzz because they collect pollen to use as a protein food for their larvae. Pollen sticks to the fuzz on a bee during her collecting rounds, and from time to time she combs the pollen out and puts it in the pockets on her back legs.

Wasps, on the other hand, make a sort of hamburger out of the bodies of caterpillars and other small animals, and they use that as baby food. Adults of both groups live such short lives that they need mainly energy food, which they obtain from the nectar of flowers.

Yellowjacket wasps are the pests that hang around picnic lunches, looking for a chance to swipe a drop of jam or a morsel of meat. They don't normally sting unless you flail your arms or accidentally dig up their nests. The friends who reported problems with bees last summer were really experiencing yellowjacket wasps close up.

Bees, both imported honeybees and native bumblebees, aren't interested in the things we eat, except for honey, and take little notice of human activity.

On a summer day, there might be 100,000 honeybees in the two hives behind my suburban house, but they never bother anyone who isn't invading their homes. In their zeal to return with loads of golden nectar, honeybees often bump into people near their hives and fall to the ground, but they simply pick themselves up and resume their trips.

LAST SPRING, a bald-faced hornet queen emerged from her winter sleep and decided that the overhanging soffit on the garage attached to my house would be a marvelously-sheltered place to start a family.

Now the place she chose happened to be right above a hook where my wife ties her washline once or twice a week. That's why Marilyn noticed the nest immediately. She asked me to kill the hornets and get rid of the nest.

I said I would if the hornets stung her, as I had for a neighbor the year before, or if they seriously threatened her, as a couple of big polistes wasps had in our country outhouse recently, but that if the hornets left her alone, I planned to leave them alone.

I do put a half-and-half mixture of honey and water in the bottom of a vinegar jug in summer and set the jug next to our beehives. Yellowjackets hang around the hives and try constantly to slip past the guards to steal honey, driving the poor bees bananas. But when the yellowjackets smell the honey in the jug, they fly in to get some, and most drown in the process. The bees have their own honey, and they stay out of the jug traps.

So I am not opposed to killing, but there has to be a good reason.

Marilyn was not exactly happy about that, but it was not quite enough to take to divorce court, so she agreed to try to live with the new neighbors.

As it turned out, she was never stung, nor was the family dog, who spent many hours tied directly under the hornets' nest. I had the privilege of being able to stand under the nest and watch the big black-and-white insects add layer after layer of paper skins until the hanging nest was half as big as a basketball. The paper is made a strip at a time by biting off a piece of soft wood and chewing it to break up its fibers and mix it with saliva. Each strip is carefully glued into place.

It's amazing to think that such small insects can so carefully and painstakingly build such a marvelous facility. But at an earlier stage in my own life, I also worked on construction projects. I can testify that one pane of glass doesn't add very much to a school building, say, but when hundreds of us construction stiffs hauled and carried and measured and cut and fastened all summer long, pretty soon we too had put up something that was much, much bigger than any one of us. Just like those hornets.

As on our construction projects, most of the work goes on inside, where the hornets tear down previously-built walls and use the paper to build vertical cradles for their young and new outside walls for the ever-expanding colony.

WHEN THE QUEEN started out last spring, she had to do all the work alone, building the nest and its larvae cells, laying eggs and foraging for caterpillars and other critters to chew up into baby food. But as the first larvae turned into adult hornets, these female workers took up most of the chores and the queen was able to settle down to full-time egg laying.

The hornets foraged far and wide, searching trees and gardens for meat for their baby sisters and grabbing meals for themselves by sipping nectar from flowers.

I happened to be pulling weeds in my garden one day when two of those killers landed on a cabbage. They disappeared under the outer wrapper leaf, and I suddenly knew why Marilyn had remarked on the absence of cabbage worms that summer.

As the summer wore on, the hornet queen laid a few eggs without fertilizing them from the sac in which she had stored sperm from her mating the summer before. The unfertilized eggs became males, and those males took to the wing outside to mate with queens from their own and other colonies.

October came, and with it the frosts that killed the colony.

But a few queens had crawled into cracks, where they are still sleeping. Some of them were killed by the below-zero snap at the beginning of February, but not all.

Soon they will emerge to start their new colonies. And a good thing for us. Else we'd soon be up to our you-know-whats in caterpillars and other little pests.

I know one thing. That big, gray, paper nest under our garage eaves will never be occupied again. Each queen and her children will build their own new home.

The nest hanging from our garage eaves is sort of like the Pyramids. Nothing more than a reminder that some of the world's master builders once worked there.

Park Is Beautiful
in All Seasons

—*Journal Photo*

Tony Leys heads down a trail in Gov. Dodge Park

?? FOR MY FAVORITE JUNK FOOD: BACON AND EGGS. IN THESE DAYS of worries about nitrates and cholesterol, the only time I get to eat bacon and eggs is on camping trips. It's Marilyn's secret method of getting me to take her out into the great outdoors.

The temperature had fallen to near zero during the night, but after breakfast it was up over 10 degrees, with the sun shining from a perfect cobalt blue sky onto the black and white world below. Time to be out and about.

Tony and I had struck out while fishing the day before, so we decided to go skiing today. Gov. Dodge Park has a number of trails, including 4 mile Beaver Trail, billed for advanced skiers, and 2½ mile Mill Creek Trail, for intermediates. Since Tony and I are decidedly intermediate skiers, we chose Mill Creek Trail. It turned out to be pleasant and uninhabited by other people.

The sun was warm as we swished along up a long, forested ravine, but the wind was full of knives when it finally caught us unprotected as we crested the rise in an open field.

Then we had heard a loud woodchopping sound that reminded us of the previous day's story of pileated woodpeckers about. So we left the skis on the trail and floundered along into the woods in knee deep powder snow on the track of this elusive beast.

After a half hour or so of wading and stopping to listen, we returned to the trail and buckled on the skis.

AND THEN I saw it.

A huge bird, like a hawk, but with stark black and white in its wings, unlike the subtle coloring of the hawk or the coal black of the crow.

"There it is, Tony," I whispered over the noise of my thumping heart.

The bird swooped low, then soared up, woodpecker fashion, into the trees some distance off.

We swished off after it, stopping to look from time to time.

"In that tree, Dad," Tony suddenly said. "Look at that. Just look!"

And there it was, clinging to the side of an old oak. It was plainly a woodpecker, but as different from backyard downies and sapsuckers as a timber wolf is from a chihuaha.

Its crest jutted skyward at a defiant angle, and its beak looked to be the size of a carpenter's chisel.

After a few minutes of posing, the bird flapped slowly off, looking like something out an old Alley Oop cartoon.

"Won't we have something to tell Mom," Tony ???as we skied off. We sure did.

The Birds of Winter

By RON LEYS, of The Journal Staff

December 25, 1977

ACROSS WISCONSIN, FROM SUPERIOR TO KENOSHA, FROM THE woodlands of the north to the snow covered hills of the south, the land seems quiet and devoid of life on these winter days.

But that is only an illusion.

Stop for a moment on the cross country ski trail through the Nicolet National Forest. Turn off the snowmobile engine at the top of a knoll in the Kettle Moraine State Forest. Get out of the car at a roadside park and stroll back into that grove of evergreens.

Stand and listen.

Soon, you might hear a twitter of sound. That isn't the wind, it's a small feeding flock of juncos. Somewhere nearby is a similar flock of chickadees. Goldfinches are still here in Wisconsin; they are just wearing their somber winter overcoats and are harder for us to recognize. The pair of cardinals that calls this patch of woods home is still around. Starlings are tough enough and smart enough to live anywhere, any time.

And there are other birds around in winter; they might be quieter and less noticeable than in summer, but stand and listen and you'll soon hear and see them. Or put a bird feeder near a window and wait a few days for them to notice it and include it in their feeding patterns.

THE FAMILY cat and I have spent many hours watching birds outside our living room window.

She probably takes our hobby more seriously than I; at least I don't twitch and hum excitedly when the juncos show up on a winter's morning. Those little gray or brown birds with white breasts really turn her on.

I have to admit that they are interesting creatures. Juncos seem to be programed even more strictly than humans. The homemade bird feeder above them can be brimming with fresh bought bird seed, but the juncos in the feeding flock believe good food has to be lying on the ground, to be scratched up in a great flurry of activity.

This may seem a bit silly to us, but it is the way nature seems to operate. If the juncos eat only on the ground and the chickadees eat only up in the trees, the two similar species can live happily in the same patch of woods or swatch of yards.

Sort of like Jack and Ms. Spratt.

But this business of eating on the ground brings its own problems.

It's easier for a cat to sneak up on you. So you move around in a small group, twittering to each other to keep track of where the other guys are. You develop a nervous wariness and a compulsion to fly up and away at the least disturbance. And you grow two white signal feathers in your tail, designed so that they show only in flight. When one bird notices something and flies off, the others are warned instantly and follow.

Now what do you do if the ground is your plate and it is suddenly covered by four feet of snow? Well, you move to a place where it isn't.

That, I think, is why the junco is called the snowbird. When a major winter storm dumps two inches of snow on Milwaukee County and two feet on Vilas County, the juncos face a Hobson's choice: starve in Vilas County or thrive in Milwaukee County.

That decision having been made, they turn up soon after the first snow blankets my suburban yard.

Their appearance illustrates once again that birds don't really migrate because they can't stand the cold. Humans evolved in warm places, and cold bothers them a great deal. They assume that that's why many birds move to Florida in October.

But birds can stand the cold; it's insects and green plants that cannot. Therefore, robins and mallards must move to Florida. But juncos only move to Milwaukee County.

HERE COME the chickadees, staying together by listening for the "dee-dee-dee" of their fellows and occasionally adding the louder "chick-a-dee-dee" if a bird temporarily loses track of the small flock.

They mostly turn up their noses at the bird feeders near the living room window, although they will grab an occasional sunflower seed from the feeder hanging in the birch tree.

These bold little birds prefer to hustle their own grub, hunting out spider eggs and moth cocoons as they travel from tree to tree and carefully wiping their beaks -- first one side and then the other -- after each tiny meal. Like a man I once knew who wiped his mouth with a napkin after each bite of a sandwich.

Snow often has coated the top of each branch of the birch, but no matter. A chickadee works just as cheerfully and efficiently upside down as rightside up.

A few more minutes to check out the evergreens, but the pickings are slim and off they go.

LAST WINTER, I finally sprung for one of those fancy plastic and aluminum tube bird feeders, the first store bought feeder I ever owned. I filled it with sunflower seeds, hung it in the birch tree near the big window and promptly forgot about it.

A few days later, there were a couple of sparrow sized birds on the perches, working out the seeds, eating one and spilling two. The birds were dull in color, with a faint stripe down each wing.

Roger Tory Peterson's "Field Guide to the Birds" has a whole page full of dull colored little birds with wing stripes. They are aptly called "Confusing Fall Warblers," but these could not be warblers. The warblers of the world had been through months before, on their way South, where live insects were still crawling and flitting about.

So I thumbed through the rest of the battered old book, rejecting one guess after another. The birds cooperated by hanging around so I could constantly compare them with the pictures in the guide. I went through all the sparrows and then worked back down through the warblers and vireos without getting anywhere.

I went back once more to the finches, and something made me notice that the note opposite the common goldfinch said that the bright yellow bird was the "male in summer." Maybe, just maybe. It was the right size, after all.

Sure enough, the text part of the book said the male in winter was similar to the female. Back to the picture page, and there was the female, almost unnoticed behind the male. The eye went back and forth from the bird feeder to the bird book. No question.

Marilyn and the kids were called in to witness this important event. They seemed to be properly impressed.

We had noticed with other birds how the male donned his most splendid threads in spring, hoping to be chosen by a suitable female. Human females sometimes seem to resent the fact that in the bird world it is usually the male that is bright and colorful, while the female is often drab and dull looking.

But that is only because the female has the more important role to play. It is she who decides who will be chums with whom, and whose genes will blend to insure the continuation of the species, be it robin or Kirtland's warbler. Female birds and female bees have senses of beauty that are similar to those we hold. That, and that alone, is why male birds and flowers are so pleasing to our eyes.

What a dull world it would be if female birds and bees preferred gray to yellow and crimson.

The male goldfinches at my feeder would wear their wedding clothes when appropriate, not in January. For now, their feathers had dull colored tips. The tips would wear off slowly, exposing the brilliant yellow and black colors beneath. We spent the rest of the winter watching male goldfinches slowly change their clothes.

Voyeurs? You know it.

THE LOUD single "CHIP" tells the bird watcher that a male cardinal is warning his mate to be careful.

Sure enough, a minute or so later a female cardinal flies by the bird feeder on a reconnaissance flight. A few minutes later, her mate follows.

They perch in the spruce tree, looking like red and brown Christmas tree ornaments among the green branches and white snow.

After a 15 minute vigil, the female figures the coast is clear and flies up to the feeder. The timider male waits until she has eaten a couple of seeds and flown off with one to be eaten elsewhere. Then he works up his courage and flies up to dine –– briefly and nervously.

I suppose if I had to wear a bright red suit in a world full of cats and boys with BB guns, I'd be a little careful too.

Birds have always been part of my life, but cardinals only in my adult years.

That could be because they are so shy that they are seldom seen even when they are around. But it also could be because they were not around. I have read that cardinals were until recently a Southern bird but have recently been extending their range northward. One theory on why they have been able to do so is that city and suburban humans have been putting sunflower and other fat filled seeds out in their yards.

That's nice to think about. Such beauty for a few cents worth of birdseed.

It won't be long before the cardinal will be whistling from the treetops again, announcing that February is here, winter is almost over and it is time to think about things other than sunflower seeds.

I'll be out in the back yard, whistling back and bringing them raging and fuming to the top of the Chinese elm next door. My neighbors probably think I'm a little nutty. They're probably right.

THE STARLINGS have been around again, coming to the feeder and filling their greedy beaks in such a rush that they spill more on the ground than they eat. No matter, the juncos will clean it up tomorrow.

Starlings are much despised, having driven out the bluebirds and most of the martins with their bullying and taking over of nesting holes.

But when it is 10 below zero, one can't help but notice that only the starlings are smart enough to huddle on chimneytops for the warmth coming up from furnaces below.

Maybe they have learned about chimneys because they lived around them for many more generations than native American birds. Maybe our birds will catch on someday.

Starlings were brought here by an American Shakespeare fan who thought this rough and ready country would be much improved if it contained every bird ever mentioned by The Bard. So he imported starlings and let them loose in his back yard. After a failure or two, he finally succeeded, and the first starling nest in the New World was recorded by a staff member of the American Museum of Natural History. It was on a ledge of the museum building.

And so the starling joined the dandilion as an import cursed because it drives out the tender natives, but grudgingly admired for its very toughness.

Time is Right to Move On to New Tasks

RON LEYS

OUTDOOR EDITOR

August 25, 1991

CROW HOLLOW, WIS. –– THIS IS IT, GUYS AND GALS.

It has been almost 22 years since I came to work for one of the best newspapers in the country. A bit longer than eight of those years has been spent serving the best outdoor audience in the United States.

But with this issue of The Milwaukee Journal, I'm turning in my time card.

They've been good years, every one of them, but especially these past eight or so. There comes a time, however, when it's appropriate to fold up the tent and move on. I was 55 years old Friday, and I'm taking advantage of my company's early retirement program. There are some other things I want to do with my life, and this seems to be a good time to begin.

Some of you have already guessed what I'll be up to. My wife, Marilyn, and I have fallen in love with the southwest corner of Wisconsin, specifically Crawford County, its beautiful hills and gentle people.

A FARMING LIFE FOR ME

We bought a 160-acre dairy farm between Mount Zion and Rolling Ground. Where else could we find such lovely place names? The farm is only 5 miles from our cabin in Crow Hollow. The dairy cows are still in the barn, being milked by the previous owner. But they'll be leaving soon for another farm.

My plans are to replace them next spring with beef cattle; I don't want to exchange news deadlines for milking deadlines. There will be a big garden, a flock of chickens, maybe a few ducks and geese, a couple of beehives, a barn cat or two. Haney the Hairy Hound will have a lot of company as she finally becomes a full-time farm dog.

There will be time to fish the Mississippi River, time to stalk turkeys, time to hunt deer. But, more than that, there will be time to walk the green fields, to watch hawks soar over snow-covered ridges.

There will be time for camping trips and motorcycle rallies. Time to visit our son Tony in Iowa and our son Jon, daughter-in-law Julie and granddaughter Meagan in California. Time for Marilyn and I to go off on the honeymoon trip we never had a chance to take before.

I'll do a bit of free-lance writing. But only a bit. Like I said, I've got some other things I want to do with my life.

Marilyn, a teacher all these years in Milwaukee, plans to become a full-time writer. She's better at it than I am. I only hope she enjoys it as much as I have.

DOESN'T GET MUCH BETTER THAN THIS

These have been wonderful years.

My job has taken me to some fascinating places. To the edge of the Arctic in northern Quebec, where other hunters and I watched in awe as thousands of caribou bulls swam a river on their autumn migration trek. To the snow-covered peaks of the Bob Marshall Wilderness in western Montana, where a couple of friends and I lived in a tent camp, ate food brought in by mule train and hunted elk until a horse fell on me and broke a rib (mine, not his). To the dusty plains of Wyoming to sneak up a dry creek bed toward a herd of antelope. To the soggy tundra on the west shore of Hudson Bay to help a brand-new Canada goose break free from its eggshell prison.

But better than that has been the opportunity to roam the green or snowy hills, the fields and forests and marshes and lakes and rivers of Wisconsin.

Along the way, I've met a few important people. A governor, a US senator or two, congressmen, state legislators, state officials, biologists, representatives of various outdoor groups, hustlers, hunting and fishing guides and outfitters.

The very best part of this job has been the chance to meet some of you, the people who care about the land and the water and the wild citizens of Wisconsin. Many of you I've been lucky enough to get to know in person, often as you helped me make my way in the outdoors. Some of you I've met in public meeting rooms as important issues of the day were discussed and debated. Some of you I've met on the telephone, but in ways that made you more than just voices coming from a piece of plastic. Some have written letters, with the writer's personality plainly visible between neatly typed or awkwardly scrawled words.

There have been so many more of you that I haven't been able to meet. But I've felt your presence as I sat at my office keyboard, and I've hoped that what I wrote would serve or please or entertain you, or maybe even provoke a little stimulating discussion, as they say. You were always there. That was the point of it all.

To all of you, a fond and sincere farewell. It has been great.

Storied Career Takes Agrarian Turn

Outdoor editor lays down his pen for a farmer's life

By TOM FLAHERTY
of The Journal staff

August 25, 1991

RON LEYS IS GOING TO BECOME A FARMER.

What does Leys know about farming?

"Not very much," he says.

That has never stopped him before.

A few years back, Ron thought about building a log cabin on some property he owns in southwestern Wisconsin.

What did he know about building log cabins?

"Nothing," he said.

Ron and his two sons, Jon and Tony, built a log cabin.

Still, Ron was apprehensive when Joe Shoquist, then the managing editor of The Journal, told him of his new assignment in April 1982.

"You're going to be the outdoor editor," Shoquist said.

"Geez, Joe, I don't know anything about that," Leys told him. "I've never been hunting in my life except once."

"Well, you can learn," Shoquist told him.

He learned.

A LONG AND DECORATED CAREER

When he retires from the newspaper business Aug. 23 at age 55, he will have won more awards for outdoor writing than any farmer in southwestern Wisconsin.

"Fortunately, I had a lot of very good friends who took me under their wings and taught me how to hunt and fish," he said.

"I deliberately sought out people who were good at various things. Let's say I needed a guy who knew how to catch walleyes in Lake Nagawicka. I'd ask around, find out who that person was and ask if he'd take me fishing. They would.

"Most readers, I don't think, suspected. People think that I'm like everybody else, that I started deer hunting when I was 5 years old with my uncle Joe."

He fooled his new friends, too.

"I never knew that," said Dick Smith, who wrote a book on fishing with Ron. "He's learned a lot then, and he's learned it quickly."

Curious people tend to learn quickly.

TAKING TIME TO SMELL THE ROSES

Ron looks for the little things. He stops to sniff the daffodils and watch the robins in the trees. He finds pretty things in places a lot of people don't think to look.

"He's taught me to look at the other things besides fishing," Smith said. "The birds, the animals, the flowers, trees. He notices all that when he's out in the field."

Ron finds beauty everywhere, even in the blizzards of winter and the thunderstorms of summer.

He was a volunteer firefighter in Bayside for 11 years. He was a driving force in the organization of a Newspaper Guild union local in Milwaukee and is the current second vice president.

Jay Reed, Ron's partner in The Journal's outdoor department, calls him "Salmon."

"He's always swimming against the stream," Reed says.

Ron's wife, Marilyn, a high school English teacher, agrees.

"That's a pretty good description," she said. "He's always analyzing things. He always has a position. He takes things very, very seriously."

A Crusading Newspaperman

His columns have led the fight for the people's right to have access to Wisconsin's lakes. He was instrumental in getting the Legislature to ban lead shot for duck and goose hunting. He has chastised those who run fishing contests.

"His feelings about fishing contests were quite strong," said Bob Hesiak, whom the new outdoor editor met when he was seeking those fishing experts. "Mine were just the opposite, so we had a lot of fun with that."

Hesiak's arguments wouldn't sway his friend.

"No way," Hesiak said. "I think he swayed me more against tournament fishing than I did him for it. He was quite convincing. I think that's because deep down, he's a conservationist."

That he is. Ron's byline first appeared in The Journal over a monthly nature column that soon ran twice a month and then weekly.

"You know," Ron said, "there's a conflict between hunters and non-hunting nature people. I try to bridge those two groups because I've got a foot in each camp, I guess.

"A lot of non-hunting nature lovers are very surprised to find out that I'm a nature lover *and* at certain times of the year, I kill things. They're kind of disappointed in me.

"I try to bring across the point of view that humans are a natural species like every other species of animals. We happen to be predators and we don't have to apologize for being predators any more than the hawk does or the tiger or the northern pike or the snake. It's a natural role. It's a part of life."

His Interests Started Early

"My dad was always interested in nature," Ron said. "He would notice birds in the yard, that sort of thing."

Marvin Leys also loved newspapers, a love he passed on to his son. But young Ron didn't grow up wanting to be a reporter.

Ron says his career in journalism got its start in a brothel in Mexico. But that's getting ahead of the story.

Ron went into the Navy after high school and spent a couple years in the desert in southeast Texas. After his discharge, he wanted to be a construction worker, but found himself being laid off more than he was working. After driving trucks and digging graves and working when he could on construction, he decided to take advantage of the GI Bill before his eligibility ran out.

One day in an English class at the University of Wisconsin extension in Sheboygan, the assignment was to write about a life experience.

"So I wrote about a night that started in a brothel in Nuevo Laredo, Mexico, with a young lady named Eva Gonzalez," he said. "It was one of those magic nights [where] we went strolling down the streets hand in hand like a high school date. It had nothing to do with sex.

"The next day, the professor calls me in after class. I'm thinking, 'Oh, boy, I'm really in trouble.' She says to me, 'You write beautifully. You ought to do it for a living.'

"It was the first thing I found that anybody said I was any good at."

Ron decided to study journalism and transferred to the University of Wisconsin-Madison. He met Marilyn in an honors class in the journalism school.

They were married during their junior year, and Ron went into the newspaper business with the Rockford (Ill.) Morning Star after graduation.

He was a police reporter for several years, but "You kind of get a belly full of blood after a while," he said. "I got on the copy desk, and to my great surprise, I liked it."

He was hired by The Journal as a copy editor in 1969 and moved to the Discover section about five years later.

And in 1982, he became outdoor editor. Now he's going to become a farmer.

"Marilyn has always wanted to write," Ron said. "She's written some very good novels. Unfortunately, she's never sold any.

September 29, 1991

WISCONSIN
THE MILWAUKEE JOURNAL MAGAZINE

September 29, 1991

BUYING THE

FARM

Ron and Marilyn Leys give up the city for a new life in Crawford County

Heading for the Hill Country

By Ron Leys

THE ACORNS AND OAK LEAVES ON THE PENNSYLVANIA AMISH good-luck charm I was nailing above the door of our new home stand for strength, the package had indicated. Ah, yes. Strength. I'll need a lot of that, I thought as I came down the stepladder.

It was a Tuesday morning, the second day of the rest of our lives for Marilyn and me.

For the third time in our lives, we had tossed the dice, betting our futures in a deadly serious game. On the first two tosses — marrying and having children — we apparently had won. Would our luck hold?

The dice have left the cup again and, as before, there will be no calling them back. The life and city and jobs and friends we left behind in Milwaukee County were good ones. Our futures, Marilyn's as a high school teacher, mine as a newspaperman, were predictable and secure.

Our new lives on a small farm in southwest Wisconsin will be anything but predictable and secure. Will we make it here? We think so. Will we enjoy farm life? We hope so.

Will we make friends? There we are a little ahead of the game. We had been lucky enough to find good friends during the 11 years since we built a log cabin on a ridge overlooking a peaceful little valley known as Crow Hollow.

For better or worse, we now lived on a farm. Our city lives were over.

Ron and Marilyn Leys and their 12-year-old hound named Haney have moved from a Milwaukee suburb to a farm near Gays Mills in Crawford County in southwestern Wisconsin.

Our Crow Hollow cabin is five miles southwest of our new farm. Two of those friends, David and Trish Swasko, had driven up Belgium Lane on our moving-in day, bringing with them Bjorn Bansberg and Randy Kempa, arriving a half-hour after the convoy from Milwaukee County.

Marilyn had driven out in the family Plymouth; Bill Van Pietersom, an old comrade from Cedarburg, had driven our Ford pickup and pulled my fishing boat and trailer; and I had driven the big U-Haul truck.

Neighbors, relatives and friends had helped load the truck in Milwaukee County, and now old friends and new friends joined us to unload the van in Crawford County. Our farm is a few blocks west of Highway 61 and two or three miles south of the intersection of Highways 61 and 171, not far from Gays Mills (see map on page 10).

It was a warm Saturday evening in late summer, and sweat poured from us as we lugged furniture, boxes, tools and such that had accumulated in almost 30 years of marriage.

And then, as I trundled yet one more load down the ramp toward the house, Trish, who had taken a break to feed her baby daughter, Abbie, said: "Ron, stop. Look at the moon."

There it was, rising slowly and majestically, full and yellow, beginning to light the east side of Maple Ridge as the blood-red sun was lowering toward the woods behind the barn.

An hour later, everything was finally under the roof of the house and we were sitting on lawn chairs and on the front stoop, eating tacos and drinking cold beer in the moonlight.

Old friends. New friends. Tired friends.

We made one more trip back to Milwaukee County the next day, loaded the pickup and trailer once more, closed the sale of our home in Bayside and now Marilyn became a real farm woman. While I followed on my Harley-Davidson motorcycle, she drove the pickup and trailer for the final trip.

Supper that night was sausage sandwiches and cold pop, sitting on that same front stoop in the light of that same moon.

For better or worse, we now lived on a farm. Our city lives were over.

THE old windmill creaked and clanked softly as the wheel turned slowly in the evening breeze. Three tall silos and a massive dairy barn loomed in the shadows behind the barnyard light.

Crickets chorused all around us, two cats prowled for midnight snacks and the air was redolent with the sweet smell of cow manure. A horse nickered from somewhere in the darkness, probably at the smell of a new dog.

That new dog is Haney, the hound who has shared our lives for the last 12 years.

Haney was a bit confused at her first taste of farm life. Her old

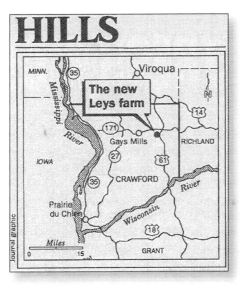

The Leys' farm in Crawford County is five miles northeast of their rustic log cabin.

doghouse was there, but now it was under a big maple instead of next to the windows of a sun porch.

She whimpered and yiped a few times during her first night on the farm, but by the next morning she began to settle in. She tried hard to keep her dignity as she met Boozie, a little beagle pup who didn't quite understand that old dogs aren't all that playful.

Haney also was introduced to Boozie's folks, Sam and Merle Anderson, an elderly couple who live in a trailer on our new farm.

She also met a very busy farmer, Howard Chapman, the former

owner, who was winding up more than 20 years of milking cows in the barn and was consolidating his operations on another farm in nearby Marietta Valley.

There were things that Haney liked and things that she disliked about this new farm.

She loved to roll in the liquid cow manure that trailed behind Chapman's tractor and spreader as he transferred the contents of a holding pond to the fields.

But Haney didn't like her subsequent banishment from the house. If she didn't mind the smell, why should Marilyn, she seemed to think. Never mind, OUT, was Marilyn's reply.

Haney does stay away from the barn. Cows live in there, at least for now, and Haney doesn't care much for cows.

As a young dog, she had once set out in loud pursuit of a small herd of Holstein heifers, totally ignoring my shouts to stop. She never saw the barbed-wire fence. When she suddenly landed on her back, blood streaming from her mouth and face, she thought the cows had done it.

She studiously has avoided cows ever since.

That was fine during all our years of spending weekends and vacations in the cabin overlooking Crow Hollow. We could let Haney run free, safe in the knowledge that she would never again chase the neighbor's cows.

That will also be fine next spring, when we expect to replace Chapman's dairy cows with our own small herd of beef cattle.

THIS is, you see, a serious venture. There will be a flock of chickens. There will be a big vegetable garden. There will be a couple of beehives. We plan to boil some maple syrup in the spring and to squeeze some cider in the fall.

But at age 55 for me and 49 for Marilyn, we are too young to be satisfied with just hobbies and visiting with friends, as important as both are in our lives. Nor will remodeling an old farmhouse be enough.

We need something more serious. For Marilyn, that will be a chance finally to devote her full attention to writing: novels, short stories and magazine articles. Her years of teaching writing to Milwaukee high school students are over.

For me, it will be a serious attempt at serious farming — not quite full-time farming, but not just fun and games. I've wanted to do this since I was a small boy. It may even be genetic. Both of my grandfathers left the crowded Netherlands for the wide-open spaces of America. Both dreamed of becoming farmers. Both tried it. Both failed.

Grandpa Leys' problem was that a small farm in Wood County wouldn't support the 13 kids he decided to have. Grandpa Den Boer's mistakes were to buy expensive land during the boom years of the 1920s and then to try repay the bank by selling vegetables and strawberries during the bust of the 1930s.

But during the late 1940s an uncle, Bill Gabrielse, left a city milk-delivery route for a farm near Oostburg in Sheboygan County and he made it. Some of my earliest and most wonderful memories were of being part of a threshing bee on his farm and of watching Uncle Bill and a frightened Holstein cow deliver a calf.

When I was 10 or 11, I spent part of a summer on a shirttail relative's farm near Chilton. I came away thinking farm kids are the luckiest people on Earth.

So, when Marilyn surprised me in 1976 by suggesting that we sell our cruising sailboat and buy some land to retire to someday, I jumped at the chance.

We looked for land for two years, crisscrossing the southern third of the state, seeking to find a place we could afford in a climate where we at least could grow tomatoes. Hunting and fishing are fun, but gardening has always been a more serious hobby with me. And Marilyn needs a big flower garden.

We quickly found out that we could never afford more than a few acres in eastern Wisconsin and that the Madison crowd kept land prices high in the south-central area. That left the southwest, which we knew slightly from camping trips years before, when we had lived in Rockford, in northern Illinois.

We were once again bowled over by the beauty of the land, with its steep ridges and deeply creased valleys.

Then we began to meet the people. We found them friendly, curious and kind to strangers. That was true of the traditional dairy farmers, of the small-town business people and of the 1960s hippie, or alternate-lifestyle, types who fled the cities and settled in this quiet countryside. And the land was cheap.

So we bought 40 acres of ridge and valley, pasture and woods. We felled 30 red pines, built a log cabin and began our association with the land and people and I and friends and relatives have hunted deer and

*What better symbol for a new start in life
than a Pennsylvania Amish good-luck
charm? wildlife of Crawford County.*

turkeys out of that cabin, and we have used it as a base to drive to the Mississippi River for duck hunting and walleye fishing.

Marilyn and I and sons Jon and Tony and their girlfriends and now Jon's wife, Julie, have spent many contented hours sitting on the cabin porch, watching hawks hunt the valley and hummingbirds visit the feeder that hangs from a beam.

So, with no more kids to help through college, with investments in Journal Communications stock to count on, with Journal and

Milwaukee Public Schools pensions kicking in down the road, Marilyn and I have thrown the dice again. They landed on this 160-acre farm at the end of Belgium Lane.

MY FRIEND Bill Van Pietersom asked recently if I was scared. A little, I replied. He said he had been a little scared, too, when he retired from his police and firefighter career. There were things that he missed, he said. But he quickly added that he had never been sorry.

Besides being a little scared, I'm a little awed by how much I have to learn about this very complex farming business.

Watching longtime farmer Howard Chapman handle tractors and cows and horses and such reminds me of my cub reporter days and how I watched in wonder as a police reporter, cigaret dangling from his lip, pounded out a murder story on a deadline so tight that an editor snatched the pages from his typewriter as he finished them.

I eventually learned to do that. Now I'm going to learn how to be a farmer. I've already attended several University of Wisconsin Extension field days, and this winter I plan to enroll in agriculture courses at Southwest Wisconsin Technical College in Fennimore, which is farther south on Highway 61.

When the cattle truck pulls up next spring, I want to have some idea of what to do next. And then I'll just have to learn as I go along.

We're also learning how to live on country time, slowly dropping our city habits of rushing from one task or entertainment to another.

In Crawford County, life moves at a slower pace. After lifetimes of living on city time, we're ready to make the change.

Another adjustment is to the idea that everyone is important and interesting.

On the streets and in the shops of Milwaukee, people look at you and turn away. Shopping and other transactions are accomplished quickly and impersonally.

Out here, people smile and nod and say hello, even if they don't know you. Roger, who drives the big milk pickup truck, has a few minutes to talk while he loads the truck at the barn.

Dick's supermarket in Boscobel to the south is as big and modern as any Kohl's Food Store in Milwaukee County, but the clerk seems to find a few seconds to comment on the weather or something similar.

People live farther apart in the country, but they live closer. Each individual somehow seems more important.

There is also a kinship with the land and the sky and the seasons. Rain is the stuff of life itself, and its presence or absence and the forecasts thereof are constantly talked about.

Silly adherence to fashion — as when Milwaukee bankers and lawyers stroll downtown in black suits on blistering hot days — seems absurd here.

If it's hot, you strip down to jeans and T-shirt. If it's cold, no one notices if you wear an old wool cap and pull the earflaps down.

People know who you are. Your clothes don't matter.

We're changing already, Marilyn and I. We're slowing down, taking more time for people, paying heed to weather and crops, dressing for comfort rather than fashion. We're learning.

In the meantime, the hawks float low over Maple Ridge, goldfinches flit over the brushy pastures, the old windmill creaks and clanks in the evening breeze, and this seems like the very best way to live.

There will be problems and heartaches along the way. Marilyn and I already have lived enough of life to know that. There will be many days when we would like to trade the little village of Gays Mills for the Milwaukee that we enjoyed so much.

But we're already enjoying our new life, and we're looking forward to the rest of it.

Consider this the first of a series of reports on a couple of kids from the city trying to become farmers. The reports will run with more or less regularity here in *WISCONSIN*. Let's call them the Hill Country Chronicles.

See you later.

Ron Leys recently retired as The Milwaukee Journal's outdoor editor.

Talking the Least, Caring the Most

By RON LEYS

ONE OF THE FIRST THINGS I NOTICED WHEN I MOVED FROM the city to the country was that country people, many of whom spend their days outdoors and are totally dependent on the weather for their livelihood, pay little attention to it.

City people are constantly talking about the weather, although their involvement with it is almost zero. People who go outside only to walk from the car to the office or the factory or the shopping mall constantly complain that it's too hot or too cold, or that the wind is blowing too hard, or, disaster of disasters, that it might rain or, even worse, snow.

They're talking, of course, about their personal comfort. There is an underlying assumption that if the outdoor elements somehow interfere with that personal comfort, the world is an unfair place and isn't it a shame that something can't be done.

It doesn't seem to enter the minds of most city people that if it never rained they would starve to death and that a few raindrops on the skin or the jacket have never been known to kill anyone. That a thick blanket of snow insulates our state's No. 1 farm crop, alfalfa, from damaging freeze-and-thaw cycles in winter never seems to be as important as the outrage of having to walk on snow-covered sidewalks.

In summer, it might be too hot to play tennis, but that heat is needed to help the state's second crop, corn, to develop properly and to play its important role in the economy of Wisconsin.

Perhaps it's because country folk, especially farmers, are so deeply aware of the larger implications of weather that they realize how small they are in this picture and how little it matters whether they are comfortable at the moment. Or maybe it's just because they are out and about in all weather and are used to it.

THIS winter began on a dry and mild note, but nobody in Crawford County seemed to notice. The guys down at the New Horizons feed mill in Boscobel, the customers and waitresses in the Red Apple Inn over in Gays Mills, the patrons and bartenders in the tavern up at Rolling Ground never brought it up.

Then winter turned bitter, with temperatures dropping well below zero. Do you know what the reaction was when I mentioned here and there that it sure was cold? Well, it's that time of year, would be the reply.

My wife, Marilyn, and I were among five country people who shared Christmas dinner and later sat around an open fire as strong gusts howled outside. The temperature was zero. No one even mentioned it.

I went to a farm auction one day. It was nine below zero when I left home. It was four below zero when I returned. I had hoped the weather would keep most potential bidders home. Wrong. I was one of several hundred farmers, and most of them had brought their checkbooks. I was outbid on everything except an old cattle salt feeder that I picked up for 35 bucks.

But the most amazing thing was that during this event, which was held entirely outdoors and which took about four hours, not one person was observed complaining about the cold.

Illustration by LUIS MACHARE

No one, no one, was slapping his arms in front of him or stamping his feet or shivering and whining.

We were all properly dressed, of course. City people could dress for the weather instead of for fashion, but most choose not to. I do think, however, that the attitude of accepting the weather was more important than the clothing choice on that sub-zero day.

THERE is an exception to the rule that country people don't seem to notice cold weather. On the morning after a bitterly cold night, people at the feed mill and the restaurant and the tavern mention off-handedly what their thermometer read when they got up to do chores.

It took me a while to realize that this is a competition, with the winner being the guy whose thermometer registered the lowest temperature — or at least the lowest that his friends would believe. Those winners are always people who live in narrow valleys, with houses situated at the base of steep ridges. Cold air flows like water down those hillsides all night long, and us ridgetop farmers never stand a chance. But that's only because wind chill doesn't count in this game.

Another exception is when a spell of weather interferes with farming or harms crops or livestock.

Last summer's nearly constant rain gave us a fine alfalfa hay crop but little opportunity to cut, dry and bale it for the winter. That caused much comment. A cold, wet, muddy spring is hard on cattle, especially on newborn calves, and is much discussed for that reason.

A drought always begins with the same words: We sure could use some rain. Then, as the drought deepens and becomes dangerous, the words become almost a prayer: God, we sure could use some rain.

When it does finally rain, we all get wet. But no one out here complains. The farming game is, after all, a little more important than golf.

City folk sometimes resign themselves to disaster by reminding themselves that it always rains on somebody's parade, that however much rain may cause one to suffer, somebody else will suffer more.

Perhaps it would be instructive to remember that when, after a long dry spell, it rains on a man or woman or child in the city, it's also raining out where it counts, across the fields and forests of the Wisconsin countryside.

And all the farmers are saying the same thing: Sure is a nice rain.

Ron Leys retired in 1991 as The Journal's outdoor editor and moved to a Crawford County farm. His reports on how he and his wife are faring run frequently in *WISCONSIN*.

A Time of Rest

By Ron Leys

E BROKE OUT THE CHAMPAGNE THE OTHER EVENING AND supped on our best china under candlelight. We had something to celebrate, a New Year's Eve in November, you might say.

We had sold our calves that day, and they had left the farm in a big stock truck, headed for their new home on a farm near Janesville. In a few days, a check would arrive for 23 calves weighing 400 pounds each and a market price of 95 cents a pound for the 12 steers and 90 cents for the 11 heifers.

There are days when one feels the great wheel of time turning, ending one period and beginning another, and this was one of those days, a closing of the old year. Our herd had suddenly dropped by half, and now we could settle in for the long quiet winter.

Not much to do now but bring the 21 mature cows and one bull a bale or two of hay a day, spread three buckets of ground ear corn in wooden feed bunks for the cattle, then feed the three remaining rabbits and the nine layer chicken hens. The small stock also has been much reduced in number for the winter, with most of the rabbits and chickens and all seven of the ducks now resting in the freezer in the basement.

That means maybe an hour or so of work a day, when everything goes right. Then there will be time for a drive to town, for coffee and toast at the Red Apple in Gays Mills or the Unique Cafe in Boscobel.

That should leave plenty of time for winter projects, including a fancy oak bookcase that I will be building for our son Tony and his wife, Jill, over in Des Moines, Iowa.

Marilyn's gardening and canning and freezing chores are over, too, and she'll do some traveling and visiting when she's not writing her fiction and non-fiction at the computer in the upstairs office.

LOOKING back, it has been a tough year in some ways, physically, emotionally and financially. But we're still here, still determined to stick it out, still mostly enjoying life in these beautiful hills of southwest Wisconsin.

It was a year that began with deep snows last winter, snow that didn't leave our fields until April, to be replaced immediately with mud constantly replenished by the nearly constant rain. Many of the calves were born in cold rain as their mothers lay in cold mud. In the worst conditions, I carried newborn calves into a dry shed, but mostly they were born and survived the outdoors as cattle have for thousands of generations.

It was during this May calving period that I was attacked by an Angus-cross cow and narrowly escaped death as she protected her new calf by battering me against the ground. Months of painful recuperation followed that episode, but that overly aggressive cow has since been shipped off for slaughter, so I guess I won that one.

The rains continued into the summer, making it nip and tuck to find a few days of sunshine in which to cut, dry and bale hay, the only crop we raise on our 65 tillable acres. Then my only tractor broke down, and it took almost six weeks and more than $1,200 to fix the power-steering system and install a new radiator. In the meantime, rain continued to saturate the bales at the edge of the field, encouraging rot and mold and a much-lowered feed value. Finally, the tractor was back and I could stack most of the bales in the barn haymow where I had spent more than $3,000 and many hundreds of hours to put in a new floor last winter.

Other equipment breakdowns followed, in a pattern familiar to my neighbors who, like me, farm with old and patched-together equipment. The tractor needed a new starter motor for $75, then a new hydraulic pump for $300, and on and on. Then, just the other day, the tractor quit completely. Fortunately, I had decided to do what my neighbors do: add a second tractor in hopes that one will run while the other is being repaired.

THE pattern, however, has not been one of complete woe. Marilyn and I have remained in reasonable health and spirits, enjoying our friends and the beautiful area in which we live.

The cattle have been healthy, and the calves were vigorous little guys and gals that were a delight to watch as they followed their moms and slowly became more and more independent. The garden produced well, and pantry shelves and the freezer are loaded with a winter food supply.

Deer season was fast approaching as I wrote this, and maybe as you read this column some venison has joined the rabbit and chicken and duck in our freezer.

Thanksgiving was to be spent with family at my brother Loren's home in Whitefish Bay, and sometime in late winter we'll fly off to sunny California to spend some time with son Jon, his wife, Julie, and our lovely granddaughters Emma and Meagan. There probably also will be a couple of visits to Tony and Jill over in Iowa. And then it'll be spring and the wheel of time will turn once again.

Ron Leys, a retired Journal outdoor editor, has been farming since 1991 in Crawford County.

Winter Gardening

By RON LEYS

EVERY GARDENER HAS HIS OR HER FAVORITE SEASON. SOME FAVOR spring, when seeds and onion sets are pressed into the good earth to begin the cycle anew. Others vote for mid-summer, when flowers are in full bloom, fresh vegetables grace the supper table and tomato vines hang heavy with the promise of more to come. And some say fall is the very best gardening season of all, with cabbages for the sauerkraut crock and bushels of squash for the basement, and tomatoes and peppers and onions for salsa jars.

As for me, give me winter. That's right: The dead of winter, the very eye of the blizzard season, the days when the mercury explores the nether regions of the thermometer. It's my favorite gardening season.

Some might disagree, but anyone who has ever turned a page in a garden seed catalog has some understanding. Who, after all, could have a soul so dead as to fail to be stirred by the vibrant reds and yellows and greens and even purples of the peppers in the '94 catalog from Johnny's Selected Seeds of Albion, Maine. Or those huge, tight, perfectly white heads of cauliflower in the wish book of Stokes Seeds of Buffalo, N.Y., and St. Catharines, Ontario.

If you are one of those cold-minded people who must have the truth, you have a right to know that neither I nor anyone I have ever known has ever grown peppers and cauliflowers that look like those in the seed catalog photos.

But I plan to in the coming year.

That's the beauty of winter. There might be a foot of snow on the ground, it might be so cold that the cattle have not dared to lie down for a month and the half-frozen dog might be scratching frantically at the back door, sorry she ever decided to go outside in the first place. But in the house, at the kitchen table, in the mind behind those eyes scanning seed catalogs from Johnny's, Stokes, J.W. Jung of Randolph, Wis., and Burpee Gardens of Warminster, Pa., the weather is always perfect.

The sun shines every day, it rains every fourth night, balmy breezes cause the tomato blossoms to germinate perfectly, honeybees can fly everyday to carry pollen from one squash blossom to another, it's cool enough for lettuce but warm enough for eggplants to grow vigorously, weeds have failed to sprout this year, and slugs and bugs are nowhere to be seen. The lipstick peppers glow dark red, the ancho peppers are just the right size and shape for chiles rellenos, the orange sheen of the habanero peppers hints at the fire concealed inside, the White Sails cauliflower are as big as basketballs, as hard as rocks and as white as, yes, the snow outside.

SO THE order forms are torn from the catalogs, set next to each other, with the catalogs arranged neatly to the left. The pen is poised, the checkbook is handy.

Let's start with beans. Now 1992 was a perfect bean year out here, with Marilyn crying for mercy as beans came by the bushel.

Last year? Best to forget last year.

A spring application of well-rotted cow manure, of which we have plenty, will bring plants that Jack of the beanstalk story would envy. So we'll order Kentucky Blue pole beans, Pencil Pod wax beans, Roma bush green beans and, even though we've never had luck with lima beans, this will be the year for King of the Garden limas. We'll also find room for pinto beans, soldier beans and this year the Vermont cranberry beans finally will succeed.

For beets, we've had good luck with Red Ace, and will order them again.

Next come some of the vegetables that must be started indoors in Wisconsin, and the greenhouse that we built in the former milk house of our old dairy barn will be the perfect place for Widgeon brussels sprouts, Perfect Ball cabbage, Sweet Sandwich onions, King Richard leeks, Early Girl tomatoes, Sugar Baby watermelons and Italian pink eggplants.

Friends from China who are living temporarily in the Chicago area drive out now and then to visit, and to cook up a splendid Chinese meal for us. Let's see, what can we grow that they would recognize? Some bok choy cabbage, for sure. And shungiku, a mustard-like plant that makes wonderful soup.

Now let's think about my favorite vegetable: corn. Whenever Marilyn asks what I would like for supper, I always mention corn as a vegetable. She always replies: I don't even know why I ask you. We like the bicolor varieties, especially the super sweets, and there's an amazing variety to choose from, with such wonderful names as Sweet Heart, Milk 'n' Honey, Aloha and Phenomenal, all with different maturity dates.

Maybe we'll order them all and have a succession of fresh corn for weeks on end.

America. What a great country. Democracy, rock 'n' roll, Harley-Davidson motorcycles and seed catalogs.

Ron Leys retired in 1991 as The Journal's outdoor editor and moved to a Crawford County farm. His columns run frequently in *WISCONSIN*.

Barn Dance

By Ron Leys

I WISH YOU COULD HAVE BEEN IN OUR BARN ONE NIGHT THIS spring. With a skirl of sound from a fiddle, a beat from a washtub bass, the insistent strumming of a guitar and banjo, the reedy notes of an accordion, and the swirl and stomp of dancers, we brought a too-often-forgotten country tradition back to life on our farm.

Outside of the barn, a three-quarter moon rode high above, and mating frogs and toads trilled from a nearby pond. Light spilled out the wide-open barn doors, bathing dancers who had stepped out for a break, and the music flooded across the hills and hollows of the Town of Scott, Crawford County, USA.

Step inside and the first thing you would have noticed would have been the arched barn rafters 40 feet above the heads of the dancers and musicians, a cathedral built to store hay but dedicated on this night to a good time for everyone. Over on the side, three sawhorse-and-plywood tables were covered with the bounty of a potluck –– casseroles, salads, rhubarb desserts, cookies –– and a picnic cooler full of beer and soda.

A floodlight at the far end and colored lamps over the musicians lit the scene, etching the details with shadow accents.

There was an excitement in the air, a joyous coming together, a celebration of more than 50 friends and neighbors, of farmers and hippies, of preachers and teachers, of just plain folks who liked each other and their way of life. Two-year-old children were welcomed into the square and circle dances, and an old hound dog named Haney found herself inside a dancing ring of people, first enjoying herself, then confused and bewildered until rescued by a friend.

It was indeed one of those magic, unforgettable nights.

IT HAD all begun last winter, as I labored with pitchfork, shovel, wheelbarrow and pickup truck to clear junk and spoiled hay from the 90- by 30-foot main hayloft of my barn. The floor, I knew, was rotten in places and would have to be replaced before I could drive 1,000-pound round bales of hay inside with a tractor.

Storing round bales outdoors, I had discovered, was possible but resulted in too much spoiled hay and many a struggle in deep snow and bitter cold to free a bale for a day's feed for my herd of beef cattle.

There was much time to think as I went about this mindless job and as I later spent days on my knees nailing a double layer of ¾-inch plywood over the old floor.

Why not take advantage of this new floor before the barn filled with hay again? Why not hold a barn dance?

And so, on a winter's morning that brought me to town on errands, I ran into Tim Jenkins at the counter of the Unique Cafe in Boscobel. Jenkins is a fiddler and Kettle Creek String Band leader and square-dance caller of some note — if one may be excused a pun — and I broached the subject.

He brought out a well-thumbed calendar notebook and asked what time of year. Just before haying, I said. I've got a Friday free, Jenkins said. Would that be OK?

Let's do it, I replied.

Marilyn wrote to a friend, Hong Di, and invited her to come up from suburban Chicago for the weekend. Hong Di grew up among farmers in China and, although she has lived in American cities for several years, including Milwaukee, she misses the countryside enough so that she visits us from time to time. She was not about to turn down a chance to go to a real barn dance.

SO Marilyn and I and Hong Di and Tim Jenkins gave the barn a final "sweep-down," set up makeshift tables, hauled folding chairs from the Kickapoo Natural Foods Co-op in Gays Mills, set up lights and microphones and amplifiers.

The news had been spread through word of mouth and a poster created by Jenkins' daughter, Kelsey, and mounted at the co-op.

Just after 6 p.m., cars and pickup trucks began rolling up Belgium Lane, parking and disgorging men and women and kids, bringing food and excitement and anticipation.

It was a cool night, following a day of persistent rain, but the clouds broke up, and the sun came out (and later the moon), the food was consumed and exclaimed over, the fiddles and bass and guitars and banjos warmed up, and the dance began.

It went on for hours and hours, until children tired and farmers started to think of the milking at dawn. The crowd began to thin, but the music continued to rise and fall, and the musicians were the last to leave, reluctantly, playing just one more piece, and then one more, and then one more after that.

And then the barn was empty again. The lights were doused. Outside, the moon rode high in the western sky and the frogs chorused from the pond. The magic was over, except for that part that would live forever in the memory.

Ron Leys retired in 1991 as The Journal's outdoor editor and moved to a Crawford County farm. His reports on how he and his wife, Marilyn, are faring run frequently in *WISCONSIN*.

Threshing Bee

By Ron Leys

*M*IKE GORMAN THREW THE OLD ALLIS-CHALMERS TRACTOR into gear. A pulley began to turn and a belt began to move and the big McCormick-Deering threshing machine at the other end of the belt trembled and clattered and then roared, and a horizontal plume of yellow oat straw geysered for 50 feet.

It was, however, much more than a threshing machine that went into operation on this cool, sunny September afternoon on the old Hansen farm in Richland County here in southwestern Wisconsin.

It also was a time machine.

The old-timers who had been leaning on pitchforks straightened up, their eyes gleamed and they were transported back, far back, into the days when they were young and strong and played important roles in this one-time annual farming ritual.

They were back once again to the magic time when the "custom man" came down the town road with his threshing machine in tow, ready to do customized threshing work for hire. Some of the old-timers were old enough to remember when the thresher was pulled by a chuffing steam engine. Others dated only to tractor power, but the differences were small.

The central fact was that the custom threshing machine typically would go from farm to farm in a neighborhood, and neighbors, friends and relatives would follow the operation to help each other at each place.

The mission was to use a power source to operate a machine that would separate the seeds — known as grain — from the stems, or straw. The crop could be oats, wheat or barley, with the grain used as feed for animals or food for people, and the straw for animal bedding. Or it could be flax, in which case the grain — known as linseed — is used in making paint and other products.

First, the crop was cut, or reaped, and dropped in bundles in the field. The bundles were piled into shocks (rounded heaps) to dry, and later pitched onto bundle wagons pulled by horses or tractors into the barnyard, where the threshing machine was set up. The operation typically used the labor of a dozen men and boys.

Before the invention of threshing — pronounced "thrashing" — machines, the work was done by beating the plants with sticks or driving hoofed animals across the cut stalks. Hence the Bible proverb: "Muzzle not the ox that treads the grain."

Since the 1950s, the work has been done by tractor-drawn or self-propelled machines known as combines, so called because they combine the cutting and the threshing operations as they move across fields.

It has become a one-man, or at most two-person, operation and the old threshing bee or thresheree has disappeared. . . except for a few very special occasions.

JUST as in the old days, shallow trenches were dug on this September afternoon and Gorman backed the thresher until its rear wheels settled in so that the machine would sit level.

Then the tractor was unhitched from the thresher's tongue, Gorman backed off 20 feet and a wide belt went over the tractor's drive pulley and around the main pulley of the thresher. The intake chute was unfolded and a bundle wagon was pulled up to the left side of the gray, galvanized-steel thresher.

When the threshing/time machine roared into life, it wasn't just the old-timers who were taken back 40 and 50 years. Gorman, known to most of the crowd as Father Mike for his day job as chancellor of the

La Crosse Catholic Diocese, was whisked back to his boyhood on the farm of his parents, Kyrie and Sue Gorman, just down the road.

I was transported to the barnyard of my uncle in Sheboygan County, where, at age 6, I watched wide-eyed as the family gathered to thrash flax into linseed and straw.

Pat Kinney, now a 55-year-old grade-school principal in Middleton,

Journal illustration

recalled teenage days spent helping his uncle Mike Kinney and his father, Jim, run their machines on farms in Richland and Crawford Counties. They charged 8 cents per bushel of grain threshed, with the host farm providing most of the labor and all of the food. Kinney said he especially liked working on Norwegian farms, where a lunch of coffee and cake was served at 10 a.m., dinner at noon, another lunch at 3 p.m., then supper at 6 p.m.

"One of the things I marvel at," he said, "was the way everybody washed up in the same washtub. The water would turn gray."

Kinney said his uncle and father were among the last in the custom threshing business, continuing into the period when most farmers owned their own combines or hired one man and his combine to do all the work.

Eventually, the work petered out, and today threshing bees are largely ceremonial affairs –– as was this one on the Hansen farm, which was bought two years ago by West Allis residents Tom and Mary Rondeau, who use it as a weekend and vacation retreat. Mary Rondeau said they had 87 guests for the thresheree.

THIS 1993 thresheree was, as of old, mostly a chance for Gormans and Kinneys and Nees and associated folks from the hollows and ridges of Richland, Crawford and Vernon Counties to get together with extended families, some from as close as Middleton outside of Madison and one from as far as Melbourne, Australia. That was Susan Gorence Frantzeskos, 34, daughter of Joanne Gorman Gorence.

The 35-foot-long McCormick-Deering was the last of the five threshing machines — sometimes known as separators — owned by Jim and Mike Kinney and operated into the 1960s. Father Mike had learned to operate this survivor, and it and the Allis-Chalmers tractor that powered it eventually were willed to him.

How long has he been threshing? he was asked.

"All my life," came the reply, and this 38-year-old priest wasn't just talking about bringing in the sheaves for the Catholic Church. He has been operating his machine at clan threshing bees since about 1975.

Was he the big boss, sometimes known as the grain boss, or was he an assistant, known as a straw boss?

"We're all bosses here," this diplomatic priest replied. And so we were, including this correspondent.

Ron Leys retired in 1991 as The Journal's outdoor editor and moved to a Crawford County farm. His reports on how he and his wife, Marilyn, are faring run frequently in *WISCONSIN.*

Photo by Marilyn Leys

Backyard Winemaking

It all begins with a few grapes,
a potato masher and a lot of faith

By Ron Leys of The Journal

AKING WINE IS A LITTLE LIKE RAISING CHILDREN. BOTH JOBS require a certain amount of work and a lot of luck. Both promise the rewards of gracious company at the dinner table. And both tasks, if they come out right, make a man feel that he has accomplished something worthwhile in this world.

The hell of it is that both children and wine enter the world in a rather raw state, and there is no way of knowing how each will turn out. One can read and reread Dr. Spock's "Baby and Child Care" or Taylor and Vine's "Home Winemaker's Handbook," but it is clear from the beginning that these are mere guides —— they are not at all like directions on how to assemble a barbecue set or make a pineapple upside down cake.

One therefore has the choice of taking things seriously or not. Since children *must* be taken somewhat seriously, else what will grandmas and neighbors think, perhaps wine can be approached a bit more from the oh-what-the-hell point of view. Besides, the alternative is to fall into the hoity-toity school of wine drinking where you talk about unassuming little wines and such, and that's not for an old beer drinker who likes his brew both strong and less than ice cold.

So, when this old beer drinker and once-a-year winemaker sees the sumac in the woods turning red again, he finds himself thinking that it's time to call a wholesale fruit merchant.

The California zinfandels will be in Thursday, he says. My God, this is Tuesday. "They're extra fancy," says the wholesaler. "Twenty-six percent sugar." Perfect.

So Friday morning the fruit merchant leads the way into a dance hall sized cooler where the zinfandels, alicantes and muscats are stacked to the ceiling in 36 pound boxes, across from crates of red bell peppers

The first step in making wine, after the grapes have been acquired,
is crushing them so that their juices can mingle in the fermenting vat.
Wineries use big mechanical contraptions to do that; but for backyard
winemakers such as Ron Leys, potato mashers work just fine, thank you.

and fresh asparagus. And by that afternoon, we're prying off the covers from four boxes of zinfandels resting on the backyard picnic table.

Alas, closer inspection shows that too many grapes are red, rather than the perfect blue-black that indicates that the tight clusters have ripened to the point where yeast can transform the natural grape sugar into enough alcohol to make a finished wine. A wine that not only will bring its relaxing magic to the dinner table someday, but one that will repel unwanted bacteria as it sleeps in the basement.

A check with a hydrometer confirms it: the fresh juice is 18% sugar. So a couple of pounds of beet or cane sugar will have to be added to the 144 pounds of grapes. That's illegal for commercial winemakers in California, but perfectly all right for us federally licensed head-of-household winemakers.

But will it taste good? We'll know next year at this time. No use worrying now.

So THE potato masher is borrowed from its hook in the kitchen, and we crush grapes through the long afternoon, a handful at a time. The sun shines, and white throated sparrows flit through on their way to Florida or wherever, each one stopping to look from the bottom rail of the old fence.

The split grapes are dumped into a green plastic garbage can —— the "primary fermenter" —— and a couple teaspoons, more or less, of potassium metabisulphite are sprinkled in. This marvelous stuff, which happens to be legal and used even in California, produces sulfur dioxide gas. The gas, in turn, kills the wild yeast that forms the grayish bloom on healthy grapes.

Store bought wine yeasts, though, have had their genes tampered with so much over the years of cattle-like domestication that they are resistant to sulfur dioxide, and are therefore likely to survive the onslaught. (Even so, it's best to wait until after the sulphur dioxide level has died down a bit before the tame yeast is added.)

Those wild yeasts, by the way, undoubtedly led to the accidental discovery of wine. Grapes are different from most other fruits in that they often carry inside them enough sugar to produce a high level of alcohol. And on their skins they wear a coat of yeast that will do the job on the sugar. Somewhere along the line, someone must have left a container of crushed grapes out in the sun, and *voila!* –– he had wine.

Of a sort. But it probably tasted about as wonderful as the mixture I helped concoct on my first try in the make-your-own booze business.

THAT was in 1957 or 1958, when Tom Schutte and I decided to make beer in his upper flat on Bell Ave. in Sheboygan.

Tom had found a recipe for beer in a magazine, and one evening he brought home an aluminum tub –– the kind butchers mix ground beef and sausage fixings in –– that he had borrowed from the supermarket where he worked.

We mixed up a can of concentrated barley malt and water and put it on the kitchen stove to boil, along with some dried hops in a teabag type of arrangement. Shortly after the stuff began boiling, a solder joint in the bottom of the tub let go and the brown liquid started to leak out onto the stove.

"Shhh, don't tell Jan," Tom whispered as we picked up the leaking tub and carried it through the kitchen and down the back stairs to the basement, leaving a trail along the way.

Jan, after all, had not been as enthusiastic about the idea as Tom and I. Her comment had been, "You guys are nuts."

When we got down to the cellar, the only container we could find was a five gallon bucket whose label indicated that it had once held floor sweeping compound. Into the bucket went the mixture.

Now we had to get it boiling again. There was no stove in the basement, but Tom dug up an electric hot plate. We put the metal bucket on the hot plate, turned it on and waited for that tiny heating coil to bring five gallons of water to a boil.

Well, it took a lot longer than we thought it would, and we emptied several quarts of store bought beer while waiting. No matter; we needed the empty bottles, didn't we?

We finally got the stuff brewed. The next step was to let it ferment for several days, skimming off the evil looking foam once or twice a day.

Jan was pregnant at the time, and every time she went into the basement to do the wash, the stench nearly made her vomit. But she was a good sport, and for some reason unknown to me she put up with us.

Finally the beer was done. We used a Prohibition era capping device to seal it up in bottles, adding a pinch of sugar to each bottle so it would ferment a second time to form the carbon dioxide that would make it real beer.

About a week or so later, on a Sunday afternoon, we got around to sampling it. It tasted something like floor sweeping compound and reminds me today of the old Pogo comic strip in which the character

Illustration by Freeman Martin

is told that the coffee he had thought he was drinking was really paint.

Upon hearing that, he reconsidered his previous strongly registered opinion about the coffee, smacked his lips and said: "Hmmm. It ain't bad for paint."

Well, that beer wasn't bad for sweeping compound.

It was to be many years before the make-it-yourself bug bit again. But bite it did one day when I saw an ad for a Christmas gift that consisted of the equipment necessary to make a gallon of wine.

Not trusting my wife Marilyn to buy me such a neat present, I bought it for myself.

The first wine I tried to make was orange wine.

It tasted like floor sweeping compound.

Later, I made dandelion wine, and that didn't taste very good either, despite the hours spent picking dandelions and pulling out those little yellow petals. A peck of dandelion petals is a lot. Never mind how many dandelions you have in your front yard. You don't have enough.

But I persisted, feeling that if other people could make wine, so could I. Eventually I bought a book called "Home Winemaker's Handbook," by Walter S. Taylor, who I believe is connected with the Taylor Wine people in upstate New York, and Richard P. Vine (anybody named Vine has got to know something about making wine).

The book, published by Harper and Row, was what I needed. It even inspired me to keep a log in which I wrote down everything I did, so I could go over it in later years and figure out where I was going wrong — or *right*, for that matter.

Finally, I asked a Sicilian friend where I might find a source of winemaking grapes. She went into gales of laughter after I told her I wanted enough grapes to make about five gallons of wine. To her, that sounded like wanting to buy enough flour to make a couple of cookies. Her grandfather, she said, made 300 gallons a year.

That could be. But the license I got from the Treasury Department only allowed me to make 200 gallons a year. Which I couldn't sell, or remove from the premises on which it was made, or even offer a sip to a friend.

Nor would I be allowed to make *any* wine if Marilyn and I became separated, since I would no longer be the head of a household, under Section 240.541, Title 27, of the Code of Federal Regulations.

I suppose that's why she has put up with me for so many years. If she throws me out in the snow, there goes her free zinfandel.

My friends put in orders for sample bottles, but I had to sadly but firmly inform them of the contents of Section 240.541. They wouldn't want me to go to jail, would they?

Their answer was to join my family. One day a notice went up on the bulletin board of the Rockford Morning Star, where I then worked, which informed the world that the undersigned had been adopted by Ronald J. Leys. It was signed by the likes of Bob Dylak Leys, Dan DiLeo Leys, Bill Snyder Leys, and Steve Blain Leys.

I didn't have many friends, but I sure had relatives.

AFTER taking a job at The Journal, my first task was to locate another amateur winemaker, so I could find out about local sources of grapes and equipment.

Jim Spaulding, former medical writer for The Journal and now a winemaker in California, helped me out. He gave me chemicals when I ran short, and steered me to Commission Row on Broadway, that medieval wholesale fruit and vegetable exchange where Milwaukee winemakers could buy California wine grapes.

And my winemaking career continued.

What Goes on Behind Closed Doors

By Marilyn Leys

GAINST THE FLICKERING CANDLELIGHT, THE ZINFANDEL glows a beautiful blood red. It's the beginning of another ego trip for my home winemaker as our dinner guests admire the wine, having been properly primed with stories of the hardships going into its making. *His* hardships.

By now, he's forgotten the headaches his hobby has caused the rest of the family.

Like the weeks his wife spent sleeping with the sauerkraut.

The primary fermenter had hardly settled in the only place in the house that is both warm and out of the way —— a stretch of kitchen carpet in front of the dryer. After consulting every cooking and canning book within reach, he began slicing cabbage and salting it down.

He was up to his elbows in brine, which was beginning to smell like the Real Thing, when thoughts began whirling through his mind. Fermentation of sauerkraut, like the fermentation of wine, is caused by mysterious organisms working constantly, he reminded himself. But, he reasoned, drying off his elbows, they are two entirely different organisms. Let them go to work side by side and the end product might wind up tasting a little like wine and a little like kraut. Totally unpalatable.

Still, both hobbies had to be stored somewhere warm, so he began looking for a second spot.

Now, ordinarily at the "Bayside Winery," problems are approached scientifically. Thousands of books and gauges are consulted before any step is taken. But the decision to put the crock of sauerkraut on a cabinet in our bedroom was unilateral —— taken without benefit of professional advice.

At least, this is what I tried to tell him as I barred his way. The odor of sauerkraut already was filling the room. Don't worry, he reassured me. The cover he was about to design would seal *out* air and seal *in* the smell, too. The garbage bag filled with water which he set on top of the kraut accomplished this beautifully. I stopped worrying and went to sleep.

About 3 in the morning, mysterious things started happening. The children were asleep; the cat was still; on the freeway outside, the cars had stopped rumbling. But the sauerkraut was awake —— and working. As it busily fermented, just 10 feet from my ears, it began belching four times a minute . . . the sounds reverberating against the sides of the pottery crock. I was wide awake! No way could I get back to sleep; there was no distinct cadence to the eruptions —— I could never predict exactly when the next burp would occur.

The sauerkraut continued these late night burp sessions for two weeks.

SAUERKRAUT wasn't the only problem I hadn't expected when I married Ron. Because of his winemaking, we were once involved with organized crime. Well, in a manner of speaking.

This was back in Rockford, in the days when Ron was still a two crate winemaker. He had decided that the wine from his grapes would taste better if it was aged in wood. One day, he passed a store with wooden kegs in the window, kegs which rose from floor to ceiling, a veritable screen of kegs of all sizes. Ron reasoned that the store sold kegs.

A sign on the door informed him that the kegs were sold by appointment only.

On the appointed day, he took his money to the store and, entering, found a bank of telephones, each accompanied by a pad of paper with numbers on it, several pencils and a fireproof wastebasket. No, Ron didn't place a bet; he just bought his keg and left.

Later, he was told by other reporters that the store was owned by a member of Rockford's Mafia. They all had a chuckle about what the others had decided was the more orthodox use of the kegs. They'd undoubtedly been used to hold cement, and the cement was used to hold feet.

WHEN Ron graduated to four crates of grapes, he bought a large plastic garbage can which was to be known, under pain of beating, as his primary fermenter.

"How are you going to cover that thing?" I asked, eyeing its large, open top.

"Doesn't need a cover," he replied, dumping in the last of the grapes. "With all the chemicals I've added, the wild yeast doesn't have a chance."

But the fermenter hadn't even settled into its spot on the carpet when the cat was right beside it, winding up the springs in her legs, ready to jump on top of the new arrival to investigate.

"––––––––––, hold the cat!" Ron cried, racing for the basement, "and I'll find a cover."

"I'm glad to see that you're finally beginning to care about her," I hollered after my husband –– the avowed cat hater.

"Nonsense," he snapped after he'd put a board over the vat. "If she fell in and drowned, she'd probably give the wine an off-taste."

He didn't have to tell me what else he was thinking. He was picturing the scene a year later:

Ten dinner guests sitting around our table. They raise their glasses to the flickering candlelight and murmur their admiration of the fine color of the zinfandel. Then, just as they simultaneously put their glasses to their lips, one of our sons steps across the threshold. Savoring the pun even as he says it, he announces, "Besides work, guess what else went into that wine?"

Meagan

WE WATCHED YESTERDAY, JUNE 25, 2004, AS THEY LOWERED OUR lovely granddaughter, Meagan Margerum-Leys, into the Good Earth. She had lived for just 15 years, 1 month and 4 days.

Old trees shade the grave at the southwestern corner of the Dexter Village Cemetery in eastern Michigan. Behind Meagan is a small wetland, cattails and sedges waving in a cool breeze as we gathered to honor this young lady. A cardinal whistled somewhere, a redwing called, and a house finch sang from a tree branch.

In spring, frogs will peep and croak, and ducks will whistle and quack. Robins will sing their evening chorus, and geese will go honking over. Wild flowers will stake out the vague border between marsh and graveyard.

The old cemetery had been chosen by Meagan in her last days, and I marveled at the wisdom of this teenager. Just as she had picked the moment to die, signaling to her parents to end the life support process, so a few days earlier she had shaken her head at the suggestion of cremation, then used her hands to create letters to state that she preferred to rest in the Dexter Village Cemetery.

I think she just liked the trees and the birds and the flowers. Now she is part of them, and they are part of her.

We had often gone for nature walks, Meagan and I, sometimes in the company of others, sometimes just us two.

A heron stalking a mud flat was always worth an awed look, and I recall how intrigued she was when we came across a patch of pitcher plants and I explained how the plants killed and ate flies.

A couple of years ago, her parents, younger sister Emma and grandparents had rented a houseboat and cruised the Mississippi River for four days.

I'll never forget Meagan's excitement as an eagle crossed our bow at Lansing on the Iowa shore, or the surprise in her eyes when we passed a line of white pelicans standing on a mud bar.

We fished a bit one evening, just the two girls and me, out adventuring in the small boat we had towed for just such a purpose. We didn't catch any fish, but that was OK. We were more interested in the fishing than the catching.

Meagan and I fished, usually, once a year, kind of a ritual, when she and her family came for their annual summer visit.

It had all started with a phone call just after her seventh birthday.

It turned out that she had asked her dad when she was five whether he would take her fishing. She had heard somewhere about such a thing, although she had no first-hand knowledge. Her dad was less than enthusiastic about fishing, so he put her off by saying she was too young.

How old do you have to be to go fishing? she persisted.

Winging it, as fathers do, he said seven.

Meagan filed that away.

On her seventh birthday she surprised her parents by announcing that she was now old enough to go fishing and asking how was that going to happen.

Call Gramps, was the improvised answer.

She did. She said, Gramps, would you take me fishing?

And so it was that we spent an afternoon in my little fishing boat on a small pond in Vernon County.

When a couple of guys came by in another boat, they of course asked how we were doing. A few, I replied. Seven! Meagan shouted. We got seven fish! Four bluegills and three crappies!

It was a good start, but it would not be accurate to say that Meagan became a fishing fanatic. She did enjoy time in a boat, but she was more interested in the ducks and frogs and hawks and muskrats and turtles that we pointed out to each other than in the actual catching of fish.

Rather than a book on fishing, I bought Meagan a bird identification book and a pair of binoculars.

And on dark summer nights, we gazed in awe through my telescope at the craters on the moon and at the Red Planet, Mars.

As she matured, that love of nature deepened, and it found expression in several of the poems that she wrote.

Meagan had an interest in the environment around the world, including tropical rainforests, and her family has suggested donations toward preserving a rainforest in Chile.

But one of Meagan's neighbors was an elderly woman who much enjoyed watching Meagan and Emma playing and skylarking in their back yard.

I often chat across the fence with this neighbor when visiting in Dexter, and I know that she is well connected in the nature and environmental scene there.

The next time I'm in Dexter, I'll ask Dorothy to help me find a local project that could use a few bucks.

It seems to me, and I think Meagan would agree, that it's at least as important to save a few wild patches around Dexter as it is to save the rainforest.

I believe the rainforest will only be saved, if indeed it is saved, if young girls and young boys become infected with this nature business early on.

So my few dollars will be invested in making sure other Michigan kids can hear the geese and the frogs and redwings and can see trilliums and pitcher plants and turtles.

One more thing: I finally made a decision on my final spot. It will be in a country cemetery outside of Sheboygan, where my parents and grandparents and several aunts and uncles lie.

There also, swallows flit over a small pond and warblers pass by in spring, followed by geese on their way to Horicon in fall.

It won't be the same place, but it'll be the same kind of place. Close enough.

The best fish of my life. Nine pound Rainbow Trout,
caught on a fly rod in Root River Racine, Wis.

Marilyn greets Ron after his month-long canoe trip down the Wisconsin River.

Ron Leys with bullsnake

Ron Leys, center, flanked by chinook salmon. With gills story.

Lake Michigan Lunkers

Printed in the United States
by Baker & Taylor Publisher Services